OFF THE
CROSSBAR

The Game Time series:

OFF THE CROSSBAR

DAVID SKUY

Scholastic Canada Ltd.
Toronto New York London Auckland Sydney
Mexico City New Delhi Hong Kong Buenos Aires

Scholastic Canada Ltd.
604 King Street West, Toronto, Ontario M5V 1E1, Canada
Scholastic Inc.
557 Broadway, New York, NY 10012, USA
Scholastic Australia Pty Limited
PO Box 579, Gosford, NSW 2250, Australia
Scholastic New Zealand Limited
Private Bag 94407, Botany, Manukau 2163, New Zealand
Scholastic Children's Books
Euston House, 24 Eversholt Street, London NW1 1DB, UK

Library and Archives Canada Cataloguing in Publication
Skuy, David, 1963-
        Off the crossbar / David Skuy.
(Game time)
ISBN 978-0-545-98624-3
        I. Title. II. Series: Game time.
PS8637.K88O33 2009   jC813'.6   C2009-901168-9

ISBN-10 0-545-98624-9

Front cover image © Radius Images/Firstlight
Back cover image © iStockphoto.com/Sparkia

6 5 4 3 2 1   Printed in Canada   09 10 11 12 13

TABLE OF CONTENTS

To Jim York,
the ultimate hockey dad, coach, and fan.

1

PICKUP PAIN

Charlie Joyce cut across the top of the circle in his own end, looking for a breakout pass. The defenceman ignored him completely and carried the puck around the net and up along the right boards.

"Last goal wins," the defenceman called out, snapping a pass to a player wearing a Montreal Canadiens sweater.

His teammate took the pass, deftly sidestepped a forechecker, and then moved towards centre, cradling the puck with his stick. He sped up as he crossed the red line, hesitated a second, then when he got close to the blue line, jumped up into the air to split the defence. The defenders were not fooled, however. The right defenceman shifted across and stripped him of the puck. His partner corralled the spinning disk and swung it across ice to a player waiting at the red line against the boards.

Charlie had stopped skating at his own blue line. He

bent over and rested his stick on his shin pads. He wasn't tired, even though this was his first time on the ice in months. He'd barely touched the puck the entire game. No one would pass to him — typical new-guy treatment. He glanced up at the clock. The pickup game would be over in a minute, and then he could go home.

The player with the puck dumped it deep into Charlie's end. A defenceman beat everyone to the puck, and he fired it around the boards just ahead of a forechecker. The puck skipped over the stick of another player, and it skidded to Charlie. He was about to backhand it down the ice, when his frustration boiled over, and he decided to try a rush on his own. At the least they'll see I can skate with the puck, he figured.

Charlie pushed off across his own blue line to gain momentum, swerved around another player who poked at the puck, and headed back to his own net. The defenceman called for the puck, and his goalie told him he was going the wrong way, but Charlie gave them no mind. He raced around his net, cut sharply to his left to evade a forechecker, squared his shoulders and headed up the ice.

His quick move surprised the other team. All three opposing forwards were caught off guard and left behind. His teammates rushed up to offer support, all calling for a pass by banging their sticks on the ice. On his right was the kid with the Canadiens sweater. On his left was a thin, lanky player who had scored three goals and was eager to add to his total. The defenceman, trailing slightly behind, kept demanding a drop pass. Charlie picked up speed, determined to keep the puck to himself. The wind raced against his face, the sound of his skates cutting deeply into the ice spurring him on. Now he was having fun. He felt his heart pounding, not from the effort, but from the excitement of the upcoming challenge.

Two defencemen were waiting at the red line for him. Charlie sized them up and decided to take on the one to his right. For a moment he stood his ground, ready to step up and force Charlie to the outside. When he realized how fast Charlie was moving, he turned and raced frantically towards his own net. Charlie shoved the puck into his skates, so that when he spun around to skate backwards, Charlie was able to slip inside and pick up the puck. The defenceman threw out his right hip in a last-ditch effort, but all he caught was air. The other defenceman slashed at Charlie's skates gamely, but he was also too late. Charlie was past them both and in alone on a breakaway. Charlie had been impressed by this goalie. Quick on his feet, and an awesome glove hand, he wouldn't fall for just any move. Charlie carried the puck to the hash marks, moving right and holding the puck on his backhand. The goalie drifted into his net anticipating a deke. Charlie immediately cut across, transferring the puck to his forehand, and drove for the far post. The goalie moved with him, dropping into a butterfly, stretching his right pad out to block the corner. He leaned forward, holding his glove almost straight out, as if certain that Charlie was in too close to do anything but shoot the puck down low.

Underestimating him, as they all had.

At the last second, Charlie whirled to his backhand, dropped his bottom hand down the shaft of his stick, and flicked the puck straight up in the air. The goalie managed to wave his glove at the shot, but Charlie had fooled him. The puck sailed over his shoulder, just under the crossbar, and into the net.

It was a spectacular goal, but Charlie didn't dare do more than circle to his end. He didn't even raise his stick. No need to show off when it was his first time playing with these guys. Some of the players on his side took the opportunity to rub it in, and they rapped the boards with their sticks in triumph. The buzzer sounded, and the doors opened for the Zamboni.

"Time's up," the driver bellowed gruffly.

Charlie coasted towards the open door at the far end, his head down, breathing heavily. Even though it was only a pickup game, a goal always felt good — especially the winner — and his earlier feeling of frustration was forgotten. He turned and skated backwards, looking to see if there was a puck lying around so he could take a few shots before the Zamboni came on. Out of nowhere someone slapped his skates from behind.

Charlie fell heavily to the ice, his shoulders and helmet hitting first. It took a few moments to regain his senses. When he got to his feet, the player was skating away. He looked back at Charlie and waved. A few players, huddled at the door, laughed as they left the ice.

Charlie stared at them, not sure what to do.

"Hey, kid! Off the ice!" the Zamboni driver ordered.

Charlie kept looking at the other players. The slew-foot was too much to take. He'd put up with their not passing to him — almost expected it. They didn't know him. But why bully him? What did he do to deserve that? He was almost going to do something about it, but changed his mind just as quickly. He didn't have a friend at the game — and the guy that tripped him knew everyone. He couldn't take on twenty guys. He'd only make a fool of himself by fighting.

"Get out of the way!" the Zamboni driver shouted.

Charlie had forgotten about him. He pushed off a few feet to let the driver slide past, then smashed his stick against the boards, and skated off.

A few of the other kids were already in their street clothes when Charlie walked into the dressing room. He was relieved that the player who tripped him and his friends were in another room. No one took any notice, and that suited him fine. He sat down in front of his bag and began to untie his skates. His mother had forced him to come out today. "It'll be fun," she'd told him, "and a great chance to make some new friends." He looked up briefly, then back to his laces. No chance making friends with this bunch.

Besides, it was totally random that he was here in the first place. He should be back home, playing with his old hockey team, with all his buddies. Everything felt wrong here — even hockey was messed. Charlie pulled off his skates and tossed them roughly into his bag. He didn't bother wiping the blades. He took off his jersey and the rest of his equipment and stuffed them into his bag with equal force. He never used to have to hurry, not when his dad picked him up. Hockey had always been their thing. He'd taught him to skate, to stickhandle, the rules — his dad had taken him to practically every game he'd played.

Charlie felt a lump rise in his throat. He fought back a tear, leaning forward as he finished tying his shoes so no one could see his face.

Why did it have to happen? How many dads get killed crossing a street just going to get a coffee? He'd never forget being called out of math class. The principal told him that a car had run a red light and hit his father.

"Hey, are you Charlie Joyce?"

Charlie was startled by the question, and he jerked his head up. He hoped his eyes weren't red. A stocky kid, almost fat, waved at him from the door. He was in his stocking feet, wearing only his hockey pants and shin pads. Charlie remembered him playing defence the whole game.

"Your mom's outside saying for you to hurry up," he said, pausing for a moment before adding, "and that was a nice move at the end." He smiled shyly, then turned abruptly and left for the other dressing room.

Charlie zipped up his bag, grabbed his sticks, and ran out to the lobby. Now he felt guilty about taking so long. He braced himself for a mini-lecture, but his mom surprised him with a big smile. She ran her fingers through his thick, curly brown hair, and kissed him on the forehead. Next to her, Danielle snacked on a bag of chips and slurped a Pepsi Twist.

"How was the game, honey?" his mother asked.

"Okay." He shrugged. "It was mostly boring."

"Did ya win?" Danielle inquired.

"It was just a pickup game. No one keeps score."

The three of them made their way to the parking lot. He would have liked to get something to drink, but didn't want to slow his mom down. She was always in a rush lately, he reflected. At first he'd been excited by the idea of moving to Terrence Falls and opening a café. His mother was a professional cook, and had always dreamed of owning her own place. His grandparents also lived here, and he was close to them. Still, it was tough to leave the town he'd lived in his whole life. He had lots of friends and had known most of them since grade one. And all of his crew was going to the same high school. He'd been captain of his hockey team, starting forward on the school basketball team . . .

He stopped thinking about that. It only made him feel worse. Besides, they'd only been in Terrence Falls for three weeks — of course it was going to take time to get used to everything.

His mom opened the car doors, and he and Danielle piled into the back seat. For a few minutes it was quiet. Charlie was in no mood to talk. Finally, his mom broke the silence.

"So is everyone excited about the first day of school tomorrow?" she asked cheerfully.

Charlie grunted and stared out the window. Danielle murmured a barely audible "sort of."

She laughed, and said, "Well that's not the most enthusiastic response I've ever heard. How about, 'Yeah, Mom, it's going to be a lot of fun'."

"Yeah, Mom, it'll be loads of fun," Charlie replied sarcastically.

She sighed and turned off the radio. "Listen guys," she said. "I realize how difficult this has been for you. It's been hard on me too. It's never easy to start at a new school. But I still think this was the right thing to do. Without your father I need to make more money and have flexible hours so I can take care of you guys, and I thought it would be good to be near Grandma and Grandpa. We've been through so many changes lately, but I promise that this is it. I need you guys to help me a bit, though. Okay? If you could just help me by being open-minded, and give this place a chance. That would make a big difference. Could you do that?" She ended on this hopeful note, and glanced up at the rear-view mirror to see how her pep talk had been received.

Danielle caught her eye and gave a weak smile. Charlie continued to look out the window, pretending he hadn't heard. The way the game ended made it hard for him to feel good about anything, let alone the fact that tomorrow he had to go to the first day of grade nine without knowing a single person. His mom turned on the radio. Five minutes later, the car pulled into the driveway of a large, two-storey red-brick house.

"Home sweet home," she said.

Charlie jumped out and headed to the front door.

"Could you please get your hockey bag?" his mother asked.

He stomped back down the steps, and snatched his bag and sticks out of the trunk. His mother ignored him and opened the front door.

"Could you close the trunk, Charlie!" she said forcefully.

Charlie dropped his bag on the ground, spun around, and slammed the trunk closed as hard as he could. His mother and sister went inside. Charlie carried his stuff to the garage. He was embarrassed by how he'd just behaved, but he couldn't help it. Sometimes he let things get to him too much. Hockey had always been his release. Charlie shook his head. Maybe he'd have to say goodbye to hockey as well.

His mom stuck her head out the front door.

"Charlie, sorry for rushing you, but we need to eat. I have to meet the installers of the new oven."

"Okay, Mom," he replied.

He tossed his bag onto a shelf in the garage and leaned his sticks against the wall, pausing to take a deep breath to calm the butterflies in his stomach. He got that feeling a lot lately. All of a sudden he'd just get nervous. He thought about the pickup game. Maybe it was a mistake to draw attention to himself by scoring that goal. He should have just passed the puck. Then he never would have been tripped like that. Tomorrow at school he was gonna keep quiet. The other kids would ignore him. The key thing was to get through the day.

Having a plan made him feel better. He closed the garage door and bounded up the stairs to the house.

2

HOMEROOM CHALLENGE

"Hey, I got some toe jam for you to nibble on."

"Nah. I'll leave it for you. I know how much you love it."

"I could scrape some crust from my armpits."

Charlie stood in the doorway of the classroom, listening to the four boys dissing each other. He recognized them from the pickup game. He checked the number on the door and looked at the schedule in his binder. This was definitely his homeroom. He braced himself and walked in, sitting as far away from the four boys as he could.

They took no notice of Charlie at first, and carried on with their trash talk. The rest of the class was quiet and subdued, probably intimidated by them. It didn't take long for Charlie to put names to the faces. Jake was the guy who'd tripped him after he scored the goal, and it seemed that he was the leader of this little gang. The rest of them took their cues from him, always laughing at his jokes, agreeing to whatever he said. Jake had a rather menacing figure. Tall and well built for his age, he had dark, intense brown eyes framed by pronounced eyebrows, short jet-black hair, and an angular face. He wore oversized jeans, basketball shoes, and a Los Angeles Lakers jersey.

Matt sat next to Jake. He'd been the one in the Montreal Canadiens sweater. He was a short, stocky boy, very muscular, with curly black hair, a thin face, and large deep blue eyes. Sitting on a desk behind them were Liam, the lanky goal-scoring forward, and Thomas, the defenceman who wouldn't pass Charlie the puck.

Off to the side, looking uncomfortable, but laughing with the others, was the boy who told Charlie that his mother was waiting in the lobby. He was chubby, his complexion pale, almost pink. He seemed soft all over, an impression reinforced by his large, round face, which was covered in freckles. The boys called him Pudge, if they spoke to him at all.

Charlie had just opened his binder to check on his classes for the rest of the day when Liam spotted him. He elbowed Jake to draw his attention to the fact, and said aloud to his friends, "There's the dude from the hockey game who can't stand up."

"Maybe he's here to meet some real players," Jake said.

Charlie pretended not to hear, keeping his gaze fixed on his schedule. He felt his face flush, however, and butterflies started to act up in his stomach.

"I think the guy's too dumb to understand you," Thomas said.

"I think he wet his pants and is too embarrassed to talk," Matt added.

They all laughed, and Charlie felt himself flush even deeper.

Charlie realized he had to do something. He turned his head sideways, as if he could barely be bothered with them, and then, looking Jake squarely in the eyes, raised both eyebrows mockingly. The two of them watched each other for a good ten seconds before Charlie turned back to his schedule.

Liam elbowed Jake in the side again. "I think he likes you."

Jake was about to say something when a man entered the classroom. In three strides he was behind the teacher's desk. He took a moment to arrange some papers, which gave Charlie a chance to study him more closely. He had to be at least six feet tall, athletic, with broad shoulders and a thick chest. Charlie was impressed by his commanding presence. The rest of the class apparently felt the same way, because everyone straightened up in their chairs and sat quietly, even the four rowdy boys who had been harassing him.

"My name is Mr. William Hilton," he said. He paused for a moment, and then added with a slight twinkle in his eyes, "but you can call me Mr. Hilton." The class laughed politely, and he continued. "I will be your English teacher this year; this will also be your homeroom."

Suddenly he broke off and turned to his right to face Jake and Liam, who had started whispering to each other.

"I'd appreciate your full attention," he said forcefully. They immediately stopped whispering to each other and looked up anxiously. Hilton smiled slightly, but without warmth, and turned back to the class.

"I'm going to hand out the syllabus in a moment and go over it with you, but first I'd like to lay out some very simple and straightforward rules. First, get here on time, or go to the office and get a late slip. Don't come in late and wait for me to ask, and please don't try to sneak in when I'm not looking. Second, please be quiet during announcements and when I am speaking. And that's just about it. Only two rules, so I don't expect them to be broken, at least not too often."

He pointed at a girl sitting in the front row. "You're Julia Chow, right?"

She nodded.

"Didn't you play hockey last year on the Thunderbirds? I think my niece Sarah played with you."

"That's right," she giggled.

"I remember. I saw you play, and I might have even met you at Sarah's house. At least this means I have one less name to remember. It also means I am going to pick on you right now and ask if you would come up here and hand out the syllabus to the class."

Julia got up to get the papers.

"While we're on the subject of hockey," he continued, "I should mention that tryouts for the high school tournament are starting tomorrow. Terrence Falls usually has a girls' and a boys' team in both the junior and senior draws. I expect this year will be no different. Last year I had the privilege of coaching the girls' teams. Ms Cummings will be taking over that duty this year." He nodded at Julia, who had sat down. "Julia, I have no doubt, will be on the junior team — I regret that I won't have the opportunity to coach you, Julia. She could probably teach a few of you guys a thing or two about goal scoring, believe me."

Julia blushed deeply and looked down at her desk.

"Anyway, I have been given the opportunity to coach the junior boys' team, so if there's anyone here who plays hockey, and happens to be a boy, then I invite you to come out and give it a shot, and also mention it to your friends. I've attached a notice to the cafeteria bulletin board."

"When's practice?" Jake called out.

Hilton didn't answer right away. "When you ask a question, I'd appreciate it if you would put your hand up first," he said finally. "Since this is our first class together, I'll cut you some slack. The first practice is tomorrow at 4:15 at the Ice Palace, right after school." He smiled wryly, adding, "I can expect to see you on the ice, then?"

"I was the captain of the grade eight team at Humewood Junior High and of my Triple-A peewee team, so yeah, I think so," Jake replied.

Hilton appeared to consider the information carefully before replying. "Would you be Jake Wilkenson, by any chance?"

"You got that right."

"That's terrific," Hilton said coldly. "I look forward

to seeing you out there." He reached for a clipboard on his desk and wrote something. "Jake, you have the honour of being the first name on the tryout list. Congratulations."

He held up the clipboard for all to see. Jake's name was written on the top of a blank sheet of lined paper.

"You may as well put me down as number nine," Jake said. "That's my number. It's always been my number."

Hilton tapped his clipboard with his pen. "Number nine is quite the number, Jake — Gordie Howe, Bobby Hull, Johnny Bucyk, not to mention Gretzky, who needed two of them."

"Not a problem," Jake said laughing, his friends joining in.

Matt put up his hand.

"Yes?" Hilton asked.

"While you're at it, you should add Matt Danko to your list. And I'm number ten."

"Put down Thomas Biggs, number four."

"And Liam Johnson, number fourteen."

Hilton held up his hands in mock surrender. "Hold on a minute, boys. First off, numbers will be handed out when the team is picked. Grade nine and ten students are eligible for the junior team, so the competition will be tough. Why don't I just leave this on my desk and you can sign it after class. If you make the team, then we'll worry about numbers, all right?"

They nodded and grinned at each other.

"Excuse me, Mr. Hilton." The door opened slightly, and a man with a shock of grey hair, bushy grey eyebrows and long grey sideburns poked his head into the narrow opening. It was the school principal, Nathan Holmes. "I am so terribly sorry for interrupting, but I do rather need to discuss an important matter with you. Would your students mind if I borrowed you for a moment?"

"Of course," Hilton replied. The door closed, and Hilton rolled his neck, taking a deep breath. "I'll be right back. Try not to create too much havoc while I'm gone. I'd recommend looking over the syllabus, so that we can get right into it." With that he nodded and walked out into the hall.

The students began to talk quietly among themselves. Jake and his gang first began to discuss who would make the team, calling out names and deciding who didn't have a chance. The discussion then turned to their teacher and coach. Charlie tried not to listen, but he couldn't help overhear Liam say that he heard Hilton had been a star junior player. He had played with the Canadian junior team, and had even been drafted by the Boston Bruins. Charlie found his tone rather disrespectful. Liam made it sound as if Hilton was a loser who couldn't make it in the big leagues.

Pudge got up and stood at the back of the class, looking out the window at the schoolyard, kicking the floor absentmindedly with the heel of his right shoe. He slowly wandered along the window, running his hand across the heating vent, until he came close to Charlie. He stood there, not saying a word, until finally Charlie asked if he wanted something.

"Oh no," Pudge replied, as if he'd been caught doing something wrong. "Just wondered. Are you going to try out for the team?"

"I didn't know about it until now."

"Every year the eight high schools from the district have a tournament. Not every school sends a junior and senior team, but we do. Anyway, the tournament starts in two weeks. It's called the Champions Cup. Our school has a regular hockey team, but it's not very competitive since most of the best players play rep hockey. The tournament is totally intense. Everyone comes out for the games, and we have some pretty good rivalries going, especially with Chelsea."

"Are they any good?" Charlie asked.

"They've won the tournament, junior and senior, for the past five years." He lowered his voice. "I bet our junior team has a bunch of grade nines on it. The grade tens aren't supposed to be very good. Anyway, a lot of the guys think with the new grade nines, we have a good chance. You saw a bunch of them play at that pickup game." He pointed at the four boys at the other side of the room. "Those guys over there will definitely make the team. They're probably the best grade nine players at the school, especially Jake. Our senior team should be really strong this year too. We've got this awesome guy, Karl Schneider — he'll definitely be captain — so our senior team has a chance to win." Pudge paused and looked out the window, and then added suddenly, "You looked good at the pickup game, so you should give it a shot."

Charlie had assumed Pudge was part of Jake's gang, but now he wasn't sure. He seemed genuine and friendly. Charlie wondered if he should try out for a team that would be dominated by those four guys. He knew bullies when he saw them, and he also knew that Jake had taken a dislike to him.

"I'm going to think about it," Charlie answered. "The thing is that we just moved to Terrence Falls, into a new house and all, and with school and everything I don't think I'll have much free time. Thanks for the info, though, all the same."

"What info?" a voice asked harshly.

Charlie and Pudge turned in unison to see Jake sitting on his desk glaring at them indignantly. Pudge's face became bright red, and when he tried to speak, nothing came out. Finally, he said nervously, "I was just filling him in on the tournament team, like how it's organized, and Chelsea winning every year, and Karl Schneider. I don't know if you remember, but Charlie played yesterday at the Ice Palace."

Jake smirked. "I can remember all the way back to yesterday, Pudge," he said. "From what I saw, he shouldn't waste his energy." He looked over at Charlie. "Why don't you try out for something else."

"We need a towel boy," Thomas quipped. "Maybe he could do that."

Liam burst out laughing and added, "Or maybe he could fill the water bottles before practice, and serve us snacks afterwards to keep our energy up."

"I could use a skate tightener," Jake said dryly.

The rest of the class roared — Thomas, Liam and Matt the loudest. Charlie felt that familiar flush rise in his face. He hated when that happened. He knew he couldn't flinch now, or he'd be a target for abuse for the rest of high school. He fought to keep his cool, turned towards them as nonchalantly as he could manage, and started to laugh. It was not a loud laugh — it was more dismissive — and it sent the message that Charlie Joyce was the kind of guy who didn't care in the least what anyone thought of him.

That quieted the students down. Charlie gathered himself and said, "The coach said the team hasn't been picked. Let's talk after the tryouts — and by the way, I'm number eight."

Charlie's response prompted a nervous tittering from the class. Jake and his friends seemed too surprised to say anything at first. They hadn't expected Charlie to stand up to them.

Jake was the first to speak. "It looks like the water boy's a tough guy," he fired back.

"I think he has a death wish too," Thomas added.

"Hey guys, take it easy," Pudge intervened, his face blushing furiously. "I mean, we'll probably all be on the same team, and like I said, I was just telling him about the tournament."

"Shut up, Pudge," Jake ordered. "When I need your opinion, I'll send you an e-mail."

Pudge made his way back to his seat and sat down without a word.

"As for you," Jake said, pointing his finger at

Charlie, "I'd advise you to watch your big mouth, or go back where you came from. The tournament team's for hockey players, and you're not qualified."

Matt called out, "You could always join the needle-point club or the chess team. Maybe they have tournaments coming up."

"If it's hockey players the coach wants, then why would *you* be trying out?" Charlie said.

"He really does have a death wish, doesn't he?" Jake said, turning to Thomas.

Thomas nodded. "I'm looking forward to the forechecking drills. You might want to start chewing on my elbow pads now, because you'll be eating them soon enough."

"I'll let you get a good look at the back of my sweater before practice, because the only thing you'll see is me going in on a breakaway," Charlie replied.

"Let's just kill the loser right now, so he doesn't have to wait for it," Jake said.

The door opened, abruptly ending the confrontation. "That's fine, Principal Holmes. I'll get back to you on that," Hilton said, before closing the door behind him. He scratched his head, lost in thought, and walked back to his desk. He looked up, as if surprised to see the students still there, and then chuckled. "Sorry about that. Some interesting administrative details to attend to. There's a lot more to teaching than you might think. Now let's get to this syllabus already."

Charlie looked down at the paper, but he couldn't focus. His mind was swirling, and his feelings alternated between anger, shock, and fear. He couldn't have gotten off to a worse start. Only ten minutes into high school and already the four toughest guys in grade nine were his sworn enemies. He would have to back up his boasting and try out for the team. And he would have to make it — or end up looking ridiculous to the rest of the class.

"You're going to be responsible for two book reports in the first term. The choice of books is listed on the syllabus, and there's a mid-term test in November. We also will be doing a grammar section, and creative writing. You'll be writing a story over the course of the year, and that will be a significant part of your mark. But it will also be the most fun — at least that's what students tell me. More about that later."

Charlie barely heard what Hilton said. He couldn't get his mind off what had happened. What if some of the other players joined in and ganged up on him? Charlie rested his elbow on the table and leaned his head onto his hand. He was in a serious mess, and he didn't know what to do about it.

3

INTO THE BOARDS

The whistle echoed through the empty arena. The players, who'd been circling around the ice passing the puck or firing shots at the goalies, stopped and looked over to centre. William Hilton stood with his right hand over his head, waving at everyone to gather around. He wore black track pants and a blue sweatshirt, with the words *Terrence Falls* emblazoned on the front.

"Let's move it, boys," he called out, and gave the whistle another blow.

The players skated lazily to centre. Some took a few final shots at the net or passed the puck as they went. All the while Hilton stood patiently, waiting for everyone to arrive. Once the last few stragglers had joined the group, he gave his whistle another blow, this time an extremely loud and piercing blast that lasted ten seconds.

"When I blow this whistle," he stated calmly, "you stop what you're doing — and I mean right away — and look for me. If I wave for you to come, you'd better get to me as fast as your skates can carry you. All right?"

He looked into each of the players' eyes. Not a word was spoken as they waited for him to continue.

Hilton bounced his hockey stick on the ice. "Other than that, I like what I've seen so far," he said. "I think there's a great deal of talent here, from the goaltending on out. I see skill, size and speed, which is not a bad foundation to build on. I only ask one thing. When you're on the ice, I want effort. That's why I'm such a stickler about this whistle. I expect mistakes. In fact, I like mistakes because it means you're trying to do something. The hard work in practice pays off in wins. So give me a good effort, and I'll be gentle with the whistle."

An older man opened the door at the far end and skated towards them. Hilton waved at him with his stick and smiled warmly. The man glided easily on one foot and stopped next to him, and the two men shook hands.

"Boys, you are being graced by the presence of the best coach in the world, the one and only Robert Tremblay. I had the privilege of playing on his team when I was about your age. He tried to tell me that he'd retired from coaching. I didn't listen, and told him to meet us here. So everyone say hello to Coach Tremblay."

A chorus of "Hello, Coach Tremblay" rang out.

Tremblay was short and slightly overweight. Only a few grey hairs remained on his head. His face was weather beaten. Deep creases marked his forehead and around his eyes. But he was no old man. His powerful build, thick neck and graceful movements made that clear.

"Thanks, William," he said, "and thanks, guys, for the welcome, but don't listen to him. I'm not the best coach in the world. I'm actually only third."

The players roared at that, and Hilton joined in heartily.

"I might have retired officially," he added, "but I confess I can never keep away from the game for too long, so enough about me, and let's get started."

"I like that sentiment," Hilton agreed. "Before we actually begin, I need to explain what we're trying to do here. The tournament's in less than two weeks, and we can only have seventeen players on the roster, which includes two goalies. There are forty players trying out, plus four goalies, so unfortunately some cuts must be made." His voice took on a serious tone. "I'd rather not cut anyone, but that's the way it is. Since we don't have much time, we can only have two tryouts, which makes the decision of who makes the team even more difficult. All I can promise is to take a good look at everyone, and I want you to know that all seventeen spots are wide open. No one's made the team yet."

Hilton slapped the ice hard with his stick. "So let's have everyone down at the far end for some skating drills." He punctuated his command with a whistle blast, and all the players sprinted down the ice.

"I suppose you've noticed by now that half of you are wearing red jerseys and the other half blue," Hilton said, as he approached the net. "Let's have red on the line, please. We'll start with an old classic. If you ever make the NHL, you'll still be doing this one. Up to centre, back to the blue, to the other blue, back to the red, and then to the far end. All right, let's go."

All the players had done that drill hundreds of times. The red players took off eagerly, including Charlie, trying to show off their speed for the coaches. Over the next ten minutes, Hilton had them skating up and down the ice, backwards and forwards, dropping to their knees, balancing on one foot, even doing 360s. Before too long the boys were huffing and puffing, leaning over and resting their sticks on their knees.

Charlie was as tired as the rest, but he felt good all the same. He had been first to finish in practically every drill.

"Divide yourselves into five groups of eight and pick a faceoff circle," Tremblay ordered. "Skate around the circle clockwise, four at a time, with your head turned to the outside shoulder and looking up at the ceiling. Let's see how sharp those blades really are."

"Goalies, follow me," Hilton added, pointing to the far end.

Most of the boys broke into groups quickly. A few of the new kids stood around awkwardly, Charlie included, looking for a group to join. A tall, husky boy, with a red helmet and matching pants, skated over to Charlie and tapped him on the shin pads.

"Hey, why don't you join us?" he offered. "We've only got seven."

Charlie nodded gratefully and followed him to a nearby circle.

"Good. Now let's get those crossovers going,"

Tremblay's voice rang out. "Four at a time, and we'll shift every minute. We're going clockwise. Okay? That means your right leg is on the inside."

Four players in Charlie's group took off, including the boy who'd invited him to join. Charlie was happy to let them go first. He was still breathing hard from the drills and was grateful for the rest. So far everything had gone well. Thankfully, Jake and his gang were all on the blue team, so he didn't even have to drill with them. They had basically ignored him today anyway. Perhaps he'd overreacted in the homeroom class. Maybe things were not as grim as he'd thought. Those guys wanted to win the tournament, and if he made the team, then he was sure everything would be forgotten. They'd probably be joking about it by next week.

The whistle interrupted his thoughts, and Tremblay bellowed for the players to switch. They did the drill a few more times, then the whistle sounded, and Hilton was at centre waving everyone in. The players wasted no time getting there. Sweat poured down their faces, and most laboured to catch their breath. It was a feeling familiar to Charlie, a slight burning sensation in the lungs, a little bit tired, but still ready to play.

"Since we only have two tryouts and this one's half over already, I think we should scrimmage. It'll give you guys a chance to strut your stuff. Again, I trust you see the genius of the red and blue jerseys. I'll coach the blue squad. Robert, you take the red. Don't worry too much about positions or who you're playing with. We'll sort that out later."

Hilton skated to one bench, with the blue players trailing after him. Tremblay remained at centre with the red team. "We have twenty skaters," he said, "which means four shifts of five. Simple enough." He pointed at five players to his right. "You'll be line one." He pointed at the next five. "You're line two." He divided the remaining players into two lines and headed to the empty bench, turning to call out, "Line one on the ice, everyone else off."

Charlie took his place on the bench with the others. He was on line three. Next to him sat the fellow who'd invited him for the crossover drill. Tremblay placed a hand on each of their shoulders.

"So who do we have here?" he asked.

"Scott Slatsky," replied the boy.

"And you?"

"Charlie Joyce."

"Well, Scott and Charlie, can I prevail upon you to form a defence pair for line three?"

"Not a problem." Scott beamed. "I am a defence-man."

"Terrific. I see you're both left-handed shots, but I think you can handle it." Tremblay gave Scott's shoulder pad a slap and moved down the bench to organize line four.

Charlie had always played centre, even as a five-year-old just starting out. Hilton had told them not to worry about positions, so he didn't say anything. Still, it was irritating that they didn't even ask him where he was used to playing.

"You can play left defence," Charlie said. "It doesn't matter to me."

Scott nodded. He took off his glove and extended his hand. "We may as well meet formally," he said. "So you're the famous Charlie Joyce."

Charlie shook his hand. "I don't know about the famous part, but the rest is right."

Scott gave Charlie's right knee a punch and whispered, "I heard about your little discussion with Jake and the boys. Some of the guys were talking about it in the dressing room." His voice trailed off and he didn't say anything further, then blurted out, "I gotta say I admire your guts. They're tough dudes, and you didn't back down an inch." He lowered his voice even further. "I don't think much of that crew, to be honest. I could do without any of them."

The whistle blew to signal the start of the scrimmage. Jake, Liam and Matt formed the forward line for the blue team. Jake lined up at centre. He choked up on his stick, deftly pulling the puck back to Thomas, who was the right defenceman. Thomas promptly passed across the line to Pudge, who one-timed it to a speeding Jake as he cut across the red line. Jake darted in between two red forwards and moved in on the defence, flanked by Liam on his left and Matt on his right.

Jake decided to go it alone. He faked a pass to Matt at the blue line, swung outside and then cut in on the goalie, cradling the puck on his backhand with one hand, using the other to ward off the defenceman. The goalie flopped to the ice and stacked his pads, expecting

Jake to try to stuff it in on the short side. At the last second, Jake put both hands on his stick and flicked the puck into the top corner.

The blue players threw their sticks up in the air, and those on the bench pounded the boards. Jake held out his glove as he skated by his teammates. It was a beautiful goal, and Jake had made it look very easy. The defenceman Jake had beaten smashed his stick on the ice. He hung his head and drifted slowly to the blue line.

"Okay, boys," Tremblay shouted to his team. "Not the best start, but don't worry about it."

The blue team quickly regained possession after the faceoff. It didn't take too long for the play to end up in the red team's zone. After a mad scramble in front of the net, Liam slid the puck under the sprawling goalie.

The blue team changed lines, the players coming off laughing and trading high-fives — and why not, with two goals in the first minute? Tremblay switched it up as well. "Put it behind you, boys," he told the first line as they filed off. "They're a pretty powerful unit, so don't take it to heart."

The second lines were more evenly matched, and the play swung from end to end, although neither team scored. When the whistle blew for an offside, Tremblay called for a line change. As the third line left the bench, Tremblay held Charlie and Scott back for a moment. "I want you guys to play it safe and just move the puck quickly. Don't take too many chances. We don't want to give up another goal. Okay?"

Charlie felt strange watching the faceoff back on defence, since he was used to taking the draw. He didn't get much of a chance to get used to it either, because the opposing centre slapped the puck directly to him. Charlie skated backwards a few feet and then fired a pass over to Scott, who took it easily and feathered a pass to his left winger. Charlie was pleased to see that his new acquaintance was a good player. He was a fairly big kid, deceptively fast, and Charlie had already noticed that he had a blistering slapshot.

The left winger dumped the puck into blue's end. It whistled around the boards behind the net and settled in the far corner. The red team's right winger, a tall boy, very powerful-looking, who skated easily with long, purposeful strides, stormed after the puck, pressing against the wall to block the outlet pass. The defence-man with the puck decided to go back the other way, but the right winger caught him, lifting his stick and coming away with the puck.

The right winger skated behind the net, his head up, alert. Charlie sneaked into the slot, and the winger gave him a perfect pass. Charlie fired a hard shot at the top corner, but the goalie slid across and the puck hit his shoulder, then bounced off to the corner. Red's left winger jumped on it and slid it back to Scott. The defenceman let off a hard shot. The goalie was up to the challenge and kicked it out. Charlie got a final shot on net from the point, before the goalie was able to flop on the puck. The whistle blew and the lines changed.

Tremblay was positively beaming when Charlie's

line came off. He rewarded the players with a solid rap on the helmet.

"Good puck movement, boys. I liked seeing you use the point. Everyone played their position, and was unselfish with the puck. He's a good goalie, or we'd have scored for sure."

Tremblay turned his attention to the game, shouting out words of encouragement to the fourth line.

Scott offered Charlie some water. "That was good fun," he said.

Charlie took a sip. "I should have scored. That goalie's better than good. Have you seen him before?"

Scott nodded. "That's Alexi Tolstoy. His family came over from Russia three years ago. He'll be the team's number-one goalie, no contest. Probably the best goalie in Terrence Falls. He even practised with the senior team last year."

"And the right winger?" Charlie asked. "He sure knows how to play."

Scott shook his head. "I don't know much about him. He didn't go to my school. I think his name's Zachary."

Tremblay changed the lines after virtually every whistle, so that everyone had a chance to play. Charlie's line continued to dominate its counterparts, and on the next shift the right winger, Zachary, scored. Charlie followed Tremblay's instructions, playing conservatively, headmanning the puck as soon as he got it. He was uncomfortable on defence, not entirely sure what he was supposed to do, and figured the best strategy was not to make any mistakes.

A couple of shifts later, Charlie got an unpleasant surprise. Jake's line was on the ice. Liam begged Jake to win the faceoff, so he could "kick some butt real quick and score some goals." The faceoff was in the blue team's end. Jake grinned at his friend and nodded, pointing back to Thomas. As good as his word, he won the draw cleanly. The puck slid to Thomas, who promptly fired it around the boards behind the net to Liam. Liam was late getting over, however, and Charlie was able to pinch in from the point and shovel a pass into the corner for Zachary.

Liam took a run at Charlie, crushing him into the boards after he passed it. Charlie had been playing contact hockey since he was ten and was well schooled in the art of taking a hit. He pressed up against the boards, so that while Liam's hit looked spectacular, Charlie hardly felt it, and more importantly, he kept his eye on the puck and stayed on his feet.

Zachary sent the puck behind the net to his centre, but Pudge made a nice defensive play, tying him up against the boards, holding the puck in his skates. Thomas whipped around the net and dug the puck out.

Thomas wired the puck around the boards to Liam again. Liam assumed he had lots of time, casually stopping it with his skate. But Charlie anticipated the play and Liam never saw him coming. He knocked the surprised winger off the puck, and carried it into the corner, looking for someone to pass to.

Jake had been covering Zachary in the high slot, as

he was supposed to, but when Charlie got the puck Jake left his man and charged at him. Charlie waited until Jake had completely committed himself, and then sent a soft pass to Zachary. The centre had managed to extricate himself from Pudge's grasp and had established himself down low in front of Alexi. Recognizing a screen, Zachary zipped a wrist shot to the top left corner.

Alexi didn't have a chance. He barely moved to stop it, but luck was not on the red team's side. A loud clang followed the shot. The puck hit the post, and it bounced harmlessly to the corner.

The first rule in hockey is simple. Keep your head up. Charlie broke that rule, first by watching his pass, and then by watching the shot. That's why he didn't see Jake and Liam come at him — and they took full advantage, delivering a thunderous check that drove Charlie backwards into the boards. Jake followed that up with an elbow to his jaw, while Liam added a nasty cross-check to his ribs for good measure.

Charlie lost it. Rather than skate back to the point, he stormed after Thomas, who had regained the puck behind the net. Thomas slid a pass back to Pudge, who one-timed it to Jake at the top of the circle. Charlie threw himself at Thomas, but Thomas saw him coming and neatly sidestepped the check. Charlie smashed into the boards and fell to the ice.

He looked up and groaned. Jake, Liam and Matt were charging up the ice, and he was lying on his back, totally out of position. The red forwards had been pressing when Charlie lost his temper and took a run at

Thomas, so they were also caught behind the play.

Poor Scott was faced with a three-on-one. Jake, Liam and Matt bore down on him, as he backed up, furiously hoping to poke the puck away. He wouldn't get the chance. Liam cut across the blue line and dropped the puck to Jake, who in turn sent it to a hard-charging Matt. Matt took the pass in full stride and cut sharply towards the goal. Scott turned and tried to hold him up, but he had been caught off guard by Jake's pass and was unable to stop him. Matt waited until the goalie had committed himself, and then shovelled a pass across the crease to a wide-open Liam. The mischievous winger didn't put it in, however. With a big grin, he held the puck close to the line. The goalie and Scott dove at him together, and when they did, Liam slid the puck back across the crease to Jake, who slammed it into the net.

All the while Charlie could do nothing but watch. Everyone on the blue team's bench leapt to their feet, cheering and banging sticks on the boards. He knew the goal was his fault. Jake and his crew had made him look like a fool. Neither coach was going to be impressed by his little temper tantrum, and Charlie wondered if he'd just blown his chance to make the team.

4

TWO-HAND TOUCH

Charlie walked down the hall. His math class had just ended, and he had lunch period next. He was getting familiar with the school, figuring out where things were and how everything worked. Lunch period was killer boring, though. He hadn't made any actual friends yet, so he ate by himself. Then he would just wander outside until his next class. Yesterday, he'd gone to the library to study, but it was too nice to stay inside today. He sat down at an empty table and began to eat. He'd been one of the first to get to the cafeteria, so he was finished before most of the kids had even sat down. No sense waiting here, he thought, getting up to leave.

Charlie headed to the far end of the school, next to the parking lot. He'd already gone there a few times to wait for class to start. He liked it because it was out of the way — no one else ever seemed to be around. He'd feel awkward hanging out at the main field or in front of the school when he didn't know anyone.

A small field bordered the parking lot, about forty

yards long. He picked up some stones and started tossing them at a large oak tree on the other side of the field. He had a good arm. Once he'd warmed up, he was hitting it almost every time. He heard voices coming towards the field.

"Okay, losers, you take the other end. Champions are always the home team."

"One lucky win doesn't make you champions, dude. It makes you ugly!"

"You want ugly, look in the mirror."

Two kids pushed each other, and then one ran down the field, cutting hard to his left after ten yards.

"Hit me, Thomas. I'm so open it hurts."

Thomas threw him the football. The receiver caught it and turned up field, pretending to elude tacklers. He jumped up in the air, spun, and spiked the ball over his head.

"I da man — I da man," he said, celebrating his imaginary touchdown.

"Toss it back, Mike."

Mike and Thomas threw the ball back and forth, while more boys piled onto the field.

"What are the teams?" Mike asked.

"Same as yesterday."

"Then you guys have no chance, Tyler. It'll be another crushing defeat."

"You won on the last play of the game," Tyler said.

"We just wanted to make it dramatic. We'll win by ten touchdowns today."

The boys divided themselves into two teams.

"Since we won so easily before, we'll kick off," said Mike, who had the ball. He walked towards the far end, where Charlie was standing.

Charlie didn't know what to do. He'd look ridiculous watching guys play football. It was like advertising that he had no friends! But it would look just as ridiculous to walk away. He decided to wait until they started playing. Then he could sneak off without them seeing.

"Hey, we've only got four players," Tyler said. "Where's Dylan? I thought he was playing."

"He said he was," Mike said. "He must be afraid of losing again."

"He knows we could win with four," an opposing player replied.

"You couldn't win with ten and a pack of killer attack dogs, Zachary."

"Just kick the ball," Zachary said.

Charlie recognized Zachary, the right winger at the tryout who'd impressed him with his skills.

Mike took a few steps towards Charlie. "Hey, you! We need another body. You play football — even a bit?" Charlie nodded. Mike turned to Zachary. "You take this guy. Now you got no excuses."

"I know that guy," Thomas said to Mike. "He's a jerk. Let's just play with the guys here."

Mike shrugged. "I didn't know. Too late now."

Charlie had overheard Thomas, but didn't say anything. He lined up next to Zachary.

Zachary recognized him also. "You were at the tryout, weren't ya?" he asked.

"We played a few shifts together," Charlie said. "You're on the wing, I think."

"That's me. And I think you were on defence. Anyway, you played much ball before?"

He played during practically every recess at school last year. "A little, I guess."

"Well, here are the rules. It's eight-steamboat rush, with one guy on the line. Three for the field. Two-hand touch. No laterals, no running plays, and the quarterback can't run. Kickoff from your goal line."

"Sounds simple enough," he replied.

Mike kicked the ball and his team charged after it. Zachary called for it, caught the ball near his own goal line, and took off down the right side. Thomas touched him after ten yards.

Charlie huddled up with the other players. Zachary joined them.

"Dylan's not showing up," Zachary said. "Who's gonna throw?"

"I'll do it," said a short kid wearing a Dallas Cowboys jersey.

Zachary looked unhappy. "Okay, go for it, Ethan."

Ethan rubbed his hands together. "Beautiful. Okay, guys." He pointed at Charlie. "What's your name?"

"Charlie Joyce," Zachary answered for him.

"Okay, here's the play," Ethan continued. "Zach and Charlie go out to the right, Tyler and Alexander, to the left. Outside guys cut in — inside guys cut out. Do it at ten yards — on three."

"Hut. Hut. Hut!"

On the third "Hut," Charlie took off. He made his cut at five yards, figuring he'd go underneath Zachary. The defender covering him got tangled up with another player, and he was wide open, but Ethan didn't throw to him. Instead, he forced the ball into tight coverage on the other side. Thomas stepped in front of Alexander and picked it off. He was touched immediately, but his team had the ball close to the goal line.

Ethan kicked at the ground, not saying anything. He pointed at Charlie.

"You rush the quarterback," he said.

Charlie lined up over the ball. The worst player always rushed the quarterback, but he wasn't going to protest, and it was more fun than standing by himself in an empty field.

"Ready, set, hut one, hut two, hut, hut."

Thomas was the quarterback. He pump-faked, then rolled to his right, close to the line. Charlie guessed he would try a short, quick throw because they were so close to the end zone. On the third steamboat, when Thomas was about to throw, Charlie jumped, holding his arms up over his head. He anticipated it perfectly, and the ball hit his right arm, bouncing off to the side.

"Good play," he heard someone say.

Zachary came over to slap hands.

"Nice job," he said. "Let's hold them here."

Charlie felt much better. He'd shown he wasn't just a pylon. He lined up and waited for the next play.

This time Thomas rolled to his left. Once more Charlie timed his jump perfectly, and he managed to tip the ball enough to change its direction. The ball flew over Mike's outstretched fingertips.

"How about throwing it past the guy?" Mike yelled at Thomas, who flushed and stomped to the huddle.

Zachary slapped Charlie's back.

"You're a one-man wrecking crew. Do it again and we get the ball back."

Thomas took a deep drop on third down, so Charlie wouldn't be able to block it. A wide-open receiver caught the ball a few yards over the line for a touch-down.

"See what happens when you don't throw it at the rusher," Mike said, giving Thomas a friendly punch on the arm.

"See what happens when you guys get open," Thomas snapped.

They headed up field to kick off. Charlie waited on the goal line next to Zachary.

"We'll get that back, boys. No problem. Let's get a good return," Ethan said.

Zachary moved close to Charlie. "We won't be getting anything back, if he's QB," he said, whispering.

"Maybe he'll do better now that he's warmed up," Charlie said.

"I doubt it. You've never seen him play."

Ethan did slightly better. He didn't throw an inter-ception. His first throw was at Zachary's feet, however, and the next one sailed ten feet over Tyler's head. They were only fifteen yards from their end zone, and so had to punt on third down. Ethan insisted on kicking. He warmed up with a few practice kicks, and promptly squibbed it off the side of his foot and into the parking lot.

Charlie volunteered to get it. He had to crawl under a car, but got the ball in short order. He then fired the ball to Thomas from the parking lot. Thomas grunted when he caught the tight spiral — Charlie had put some serious heat on the throw.

The other team huddled. Charlie lined up to rush. He felt a hand on his shoulder.

"You ever quartered before?" Zachary said.

"A little," he said.

"How about you take over for the next set of downs."

Charlie felt uneasy. "I think Ethan's set on playing QB."

"Good for him. I'm tired of playing on my own ten-yard line, and watching the ball hit my feet when I'm wide open."

Charlie was about to tell him not to bother. He didn't want Ethan to be mad at him — he had enough enemies. But Zachary took off to cover his man before he had the chance.

Thomas didn't fool around. He tossed a strike to Mike to take them to the five-yard line. Then he rolled to his left and threw across his body to a player cutting back the other way.

"That's 14–zip, for those of you keeping score. Let us know when you plan to complete a pass, and we'll start trying," Mike taunted Charlie's team.

They lined up for the kickoff.

"Ethan," Zachary called out. "How about we give Charlie a chance to quarterback?"

"I'm just warming up," he said. "We'll drive down the field this time."

"Let's just give him one try. I've seen him play before. He's got a good arm. And besides, we could use your speed on the outside."

That quieted Ethan, but he still didn't look happy. He glared at Charlie briefly. Charlie wished Zachary hadn't done that. He also wondered why Zachary said he'd seen him play before. That wasn't true.

After the kickoff, Charlie knelt down on one knee in the huddle, and cleared a patch of earth. With his finger he drew the play. "Ethan, you switch positions with Zachary. Run a ten-yard buttonhook. Zachary, cut around him and run a corner route, about fifteen yards. Alexander and Tyler, do the same thing on the other side. On two."

Charlie snapped the ball and faded back. He looked left, and then rolled to his right. Ethan had run a lack-lustre route, but Zachary was really moving and had beaten the defender. He threw the ball towards the side-lines. Zachary caught the ball in mid-stride, and set off downfield and into the end zone.

"Nice toss," Tyler said.

"Something tells me we've found a new quarter-back," Alexander added.

Ethan didn't say anything. He went back to the line and called for the ball.

Zachary ignored him. "I don't suppose you can kick," he said, throwing the ball to Charlie.

"I'll give it a try."

Ethan had assumed *he* would kick. With a deep scowl, arms crossed, he moved aside.

Thud.

The ball soared high into the air.

"I got it," Mike called. He misjudged Charlie's towering kick, however, and the ball went over his head, slamming into the ground and through the end zone.

"Awesome kick," Tyler said, offering a high-five. Charlie ran up with the others to play defence.

"Hey, little boys. Get ready for some real football players."

Charlie saw Jake and Liam sprinting towards them. He groaned. Just when things were starting to go well.

Jake joined Mike's team and Liam came onto Charlie's side. Liam barely acknowledged him. He lined up opposite Jake. Charlie went back as rusher.

"Can this guy count to eight?" Jake said, pointing at Charlie.

"No. He goes to four twice," Liam said.

The ball was snapped and the receivers took off. Charlie fumed while he counted. Those guys never missed a chance to abuse him. Grade nine was shaping up to be a nightmare.

Thomas completed two short passes, one to Jake and the other to Mike. On third down, they still needed twenty-five yards for a score. The bell rang to end the lunch period. "Last play," Mike called.

Charlie steeled himself for a final rush. He desperately wanted to prevent a touchdown and shut Jake up. The ball was snapped and Charlie started counting.

"Six steamboat, seven steamboat, eight steamboat."

His teammates had done a good job. Thomas hadn't found anyone open. At eight, he rushed in. Thomas tried to spin away, but Charlie wasn't fooled. He kept coming and touched Thomas in the back.

"I got you," he said.

"One hand only," Thomas said.

He hurled the ball to the corner of the end zone. Jake pushed Liam aside and jumped up to catch it.

"Major TD action," he said, spiking the ball. "In your face, dude."

"Pass interference," Liam said.

"The ref didn't call it, so no foul."

Charlie interrupted. "I touched him before he threw it. No TD."

"No chance. You only got me with one hand," Thomas said.

"I got you with both, right in the back."

"One hand — and besides, you crossed the line before eight," Thomas said.

"I did not," he said. "I got you."

"You're dreaming."

Liam saw a chance to pick on Charlie, and immediately changed his tune.

"I never saw you touch him. You missed when he spun. And you gotta learn to count, cause you crossed at seven," he said.

"How can you tell? You were halfway down the field."

"I was close enough to tell that you didn't come near him."

"You wanna win that bad," he said to Thomas, "then fine."

"Do you need to have a good cry?" Jake said.

"I need to go to class," he shot back.

Charlie headed to the school. He barely held his temper in check. All he wanted to do was wipe that smug look off Jake's face — and Liam's too. Thomas was just a liar. Charlie sacked him. What kind of guy cheats playing touch football at lunch?

"Wait up, Charlie."

Zachary walked up beside him.

"I saw it all," he said. "You got him — and he knows it."

"Who cares," Charlie said. "It's just stupid."

"It's irritating, that's what. You sacked him — and it was pass interference on Jake. No way that's a TD. They act like it's their game and they can do whatever they want."

Charlie looked at Zachary with new respect. He changed the subject. "I assume you made the second tryout for the hockey team," he said.

"I assume you did too," Zachary said.

"I did. I got lucky, though. I made a stupid play during scrimmage and cost a goal."

"No big deal," Zachary shrugged. "You'll make it. It might be a weird year, because from what I saw on the first tryout this team could have a lot of kids from grade nine."

They reached the front doors.

"What class you got?" Charlie asked.

"Apparently, I need to learn some math. What about you?"

"I've got science."

"We have an exciting afternoon ahead of us."

Charlie laughed. "I'll see you at the tryout."

Zachary turned a corner and went down a hall. He seemed like a good guy, Charlie thought. He hoped they'd be on the same team again for the scrimmage. Just then the bell sounded signalling the start of classes. He took off for his locker to get his books. His teacher has already warned him about being late.

5

THE FINAL STRAW

The dressing room door was open. Charlie heard the guys laughing and shouting at each other. He usually relished the locker room banter. That was part of the fun of playing. Not here, though. To him this was hostile territory. No friends here. He was an outsider.

Charlie walked in feeling self-conscious. Jake, Matt and Liam sat together at the far end. Mike was near the door. He chose Mike, and threw his bag next to him.

"There's room on the other side," Mike said with a sneer.

"Sorry," Charlie muttered, quickly unzipping his bag.

Mike growled quietly and shook his head, but he pushed over to give Charlie some space. Charlie tried to appear nonchalant, but inside he fought to stay relaxed and look cool. He would have given almost anything to be somewhere other than in this dressing room. Nothing to do about it now, he told himself, pulling his skates out.

As he bent over to dig out his hockey pants, a ball

of plastic hockey tape hit Charlie squarely on the top of his head. At the far end of the room, Jake, Matt and Liam buried their heads in their bags. Each of them was trying hard not to laugh, and not doing a very good job of it. Most of the other boys laughed out loud. Scott, Zachary and Pudge were the only ones who didn't join in. Scott scowled at the three perpetrators, and Zachary slammed his foot into his skates. Pudge looked down at the floor.

Charlie saw the ball of tape on the floor. He reached down and picked it up, tossing it in the air a few times before dropping it into his bag. He didn't say a word, just continued to get ready for practice. Out of the corner of his eye, he noticed Jake reach over and give Matt a high-five. Charlie guessed that Matt had thrown it.

Out on the ice Charlie raced around the rink at top speed, whipping past the other players. He cut crisply behind one net, digging his edges in, pushing off with each step to maintain his speed. He didn't really know why he was doing it. The coaches weren't even on the ice, and everyone else was content to dawdle along or take shots on the goalies. He just felt the need to go full out.

The ball of tape was the final straw. He'd had enough. Since his arrival in Terrence Falls he'd felt as if he'd been under constant surveillance, worried about his every move and every word, afraid he'd do or say the wrong thing. The tape ball showed how well that strategy was working. Guys were now throwing things at his head — and openly laughing at him. Maybe it was a weird way to look at things, but Charlie almost felt grateful to Matt. He'd shown him that his problems weren't going to disappear on their own. He had to stand up for himself — and he had to do it now.

Hilton's whistle blew, and the boys stopped and hustled over to the bench. He greeted them warmly and said, "Okay, fellas. We're into it now. As I said, I can only dress fifteen skaters and two goalies for the tournament, and I think all of you are good enough to play. Unfortunately, there are still twenty-eight of you, so that means one goalie and twelve skaters will have to be cut.

"All I can say is give it your best, and good luck. I'm going to let Coach Tremblay run you through your paces, so I can sit here and watch."

"Let's go," Tremblay barked. "Everyone line up at the far end, and I'll try to remember a few skating drills."

Charlie learned quickly that Tremblay had a good memory. Twenty minutes later, after a dizzying array of drills that left him gasping for air, Tremblay blew his whistle. "I think we should include some pucks, to see if you guys can actually play this game," he said.

Charlie laughed. He was beginning to warm to him. Coach Tremblay was always friendly, always offering encouragement or some good-natured advice. More important, behind his joking and laid-back attitude lay a deep well of hockey knowledge, and there's no better way for a coach to earn a player's respect than to have that.

"I think this is the perfect time for the neutral zone one-on-one drill. What do you think?"

Charlie and the others answered his question with a sea of blank stares.

"I'll take that as a yes, and explain the drill."

He retrieved a small clipboard from the bench. "These things are great," he said, holding up the clipboard. "I wish I had 'em when I started coaching. You hold your papers on the front, and on the back are the rink markings, and you can use a marker on it. Isn't that amazing?"

Again, his question garnered no response. "I'll take that as another yes," he chuckled. "Anyway, here's the drill."

Tremblay sketched out the drill rapidly on the back of the clipboard with a well-practised hand.

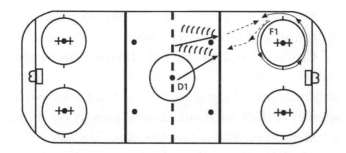

"D1 is the defenceman and F1, the forward. D1 starts at centre and F1 against the boards at the hash marks. D1 skates hard to the blue line where he takes a pass from F1. D1 then skates backwards with the puck to the red line, and while he's doing that F1 skates around the circle. D1 skates back to the blue line and passes to F1 when he's finished the circle. Then they go one-on-one to the other end. Everyone understand?"

The players all nodded.

"Let's divide into two groups, one at each end. Those of you who played defence last scrimmage may as well stay on defence. Goalies, you can organize yourselves, but let's have at least one of you in each net. Okay, let's go."

A confusing few minutes passed as the players tried the drill, not exactly sure of what they were supposed to do. Tremblay calmly explained it over again, until they eventually figured it out, and the drill began to go smoothly.

Charlie had joined one group of defencemen. Jake, Matt and Liam were among the forwards facing that group. When he saw Matt ready to go, he went to the front, budding ahead of Thomas.

"Hey, you're kidding, right? I'm next. Get to the back."

"You can go next," Charlie replied icily, "as long as it's after me."

Thomas grunted in surprise, then shouted "Hey, Matt, show this loser how to play the game."

Charlie ignored him and got ready. Coach Tremblay waved at him to begin, and he skated hard to the blue line to take an equally hard pass from Matt. He was certain Matt would want to show off in front of his friends by deking him out and scoring, so he probably wouldn't be focused on the first part of the drill. That's when he'd make his move.

Once Matt finished circling, Charlie hesitated with the puck slightly before passing to close the gap between them. He then made as if to turn and skate back towards his own end to get in position to defend. Matt accepted the pass, lowering his head momentarily to gather steam. Charlie had no intention of defending, however. He didn't retreat one inch, and when Matt crossed the blue line, Charlie took two steps forward and smashed his shoulder into Matt's chest.

Matt flopped to the ice like a sack of potatoes, landing full on his back. Charlie leaned over his prone body and said, "Thanks for the tape, I really needed some." He then passed the puck to Thomas nonchalantly, as if nothing out of the ordinary had happened.

Fortunately, he glanced over at the forwards before rejoining the defence line. Jake and Liam were charging after him. As they got close, Charlie jumped to the side and sent a left hook into Liam's chin, knocking him off balance and sending him tumbling to the ice. Jake wheeled around and waded in with a windmill of punches. Charlie held nothing back, and threw as many punches of his own. His father had been an amateur boxer, and had taught Charlie the rudiments of self-defence. So, although Jake was bigger, Charlie was able to land a few solid blows.

Liam had jumped to his feet and was coming at Charlie, but before he could do any damage, Scott corralled him and threw him to the ice. Thomas went after Charlie next, but was headed off by Zachary.

By this time, the two coaches were in the middle trying to break up the fights. Hilton grabbed Jake by the waist, picking him up as if he weighed just ten pounds, and carried him to the players' bench. Jake struggled to break free, but he had as much chance of that as pushing over a full-grown oak tree. Tremblay took hold of Charlie's sweater, but let go when he saw Charlie had no intention of persisting. In fact, Charlie was in a state of shock. He couldn't believe what had just happened. Tremblay went over to Matt to help him up and see if he was hurt.

"Go to the bench — all of you — and I mean right now!" Hilton roared, pointing at the combatants. "The rest of you, continue the drill."

Jake, Liam and Thomas came over and sat at one end of the bench. Charlie, Scott and Zachary sat at the other.

Hilton skated over. "A little intensity is a good thing," he said quietly. "This, however, would be an example of way too much intensity." He stopped abruptly. "It's kind of difficult to talk to you when you're at opposite ends of the bench. How about we compromise and meet in the middle?"

The two groups shuffled over, still maintaining a healthy distance.

"I guess that's good enough," Hilton said. He leaned in closer, removing his hockey gloves and laying them on top of the boards. "Guys, I don't think I need to tell you how inappropriate that was. I realize emotions are running high. You're all good players, and you have a good chance of making the team. But I've got to be honest with you. If I'm not convinced that this incident will be forgotten, then I don't think

I can offer any of you a spot on the team. The competition is tough enough without us beating each other up."

Shamefaced and downhearted, Charlie had to force himself to listen. He knew he was gone after this. He'd instigated the fight. It was his fault. Hilton didn't seem the type to tolerate brawls at practice. All he'd wanted to do was stand up for himself, but he'd just gone and made things ten times worse.

"You each need to make a decision," Hilton continued. "You need to decide if this little feud is going to be a problem. If it is, then you may as well head to the dressing room right now. Or you can shake hands, and I'll chalk it up to your competitive spirit. You decide, but make it quick."

For a moment the six boys sat still. Charlie felt sick. He knew Jake, Liam and Thomas would never shake hands with him. It was over. Suddenly, Scott reached over and extended his hand to Jake.

"Hey, guys, sorry about this. I just lost my temper. I'm happy to forget about it."

Jake stared back at Scott. He thrust his chin out and bit down on his lower lip. Then with a shrug, he shook Scott's hand, and Liam and Thomas did the same. Charlie then extended his hand. Matt was the first to take it. Jake hesitated briefly, but shook his as well. Liam gave Charlie's palm a slap. Once they'd all shaken hands, the six players turned to see what their coach would say.

Hilton chuckled, as if something funny had just

occurred to him. "Get back out there," he ordered, "and try to make the team."

The boys clambered over the boards. Charlie rejoined the drill, but the whistle blew before his turn. "Scrimmage," Hilton shouted.

Charlie skated to the red bench. He'd gotten lucky — no doubt about that. He still had a chance to make the team. The coach had gone easy on them. Mess up again, he told himself, and his luck would certainly run out.

6

ON BOARD

"We've only got a little time left, guys," Hilton called out, "so maximum effort from here on in."

Charlie took a seat on the bench. Scott sprinted to the boards, hopped over and sat next to him, with a silly grin on his face.

"Let me tell you, Joyce," he said in a relaxed, friendly tone. "Seeing you hammer Matt would have been worth not making this team, believe me." He laughed deeply and punched Charlie on the shoulder pad.

Charlie joined in, and said, "I don't know if that was the smartest thing to do, but I admit it felt good."

Scott laughed even louder, slapping his knee with his glove.

"Thanks for hauling Liam off me," Charlie said, looking Scott squarely in the eyes. "Hopefully, I'll have the chance to return the favour."

"Hopefully, you'll get the chance while I'm pummelling Jake," he whispered. He chuckled at the thought, and Charlie couldn't help but do the same. He found Scott's good humour infectious, and he was beginning to really like his defence partner. Always laughing and joking around, Scott didn't seem to take things too seriously. But he also got the feeling that deep down Scott was someone he could trust.

Tremblay interrupted with a light knock on each of their helmets. "It's nice to see your little tussle didn't dampen your good spirits," he said with a chuckle. Scott and Charlie grinned back at him. "I've been thinking," he continued, looking over at Charlie, "that perhaps our friend here is more comfortable playing forward." He paused, and asked, "Am I right about that?"

Charlie nodded eagerly. "To be honest, I've always played centre," he said. He didn't want to diss Scott, and so added quickly, "but I really like playing with Scott, so defence is fine."

Tremblay nodded and put an arm around Charlie's shoulders. "I appreciate that, son. It shows loyalty. But I'll be honest. You play defence like a centre, so if you really want to help the team, and not make Scott cover three quarters of the ice in his own end, how about moving up? I'll just find another partner for Scott — someone who is more comfortable playing defence — and we'll be set."

Tremblay went off to the far end of the bench and returned with another player. "Boys, say hello to Nick."

"Hello, Nick," Charlie and Scott said in unison.

"Nick was playing right wing, when all along he wanted to play defence. How about a switch?"

"Sounds good to me," Nick said. "You look familiar," he said to Scott as he sat down.

"It could be because we've been going to the same school since grade one."

Nick shook his head. "I don't think that's it."

"I'm a huge movie star," Scott said.

"Maybe that's it."

Scott held out his glove to Charlie, who gave it a punch with his own. "You go score some goals," Scott said good-naturedly. As he was leaving, he heard Scott wisecrack to Nick, "I didn't have the heart to tell him that a defenceman tries to stop the other team from scoring."

Charlie shook his head. He knew he'd never get the last word in with him.

Tremblay had pushed apart two players, and was pointing for him to sit between them. "Meet your new centre," Tremblay said. Then the puck was dropped to start the scrimmage, so he left it at that and turned his attention to the game.

Charlie was glad to see that Zachary was one of his new linemates. Charlie didn't know the other winger's name, although if memory served him, he wasn't the strongest player.

"It was about time you did that," Zachary said.

"Maybe," he replied. "I hope I didn't cost you a spot on the team."

"Can't worry about that now."

Charlie reached down for a water bottle. He'd barely taken a sip when the whistle blew and Tremblay told his line to change it up. All three boys hopped the boards and made their way for a faceoff in their end, to the goalie's left. Scott and Nick also came on, and once Scott was in position he begged Charlie to pull it back.

Mike was lined up for the draw. Charlie had spent countless hours practising faceoffs in the basement of his old house. His sister would drop the puck, and he and his father would battle it out. They used to keep score, first to fifty won. Last year Charlie had begun to win more than he lost, so he was fairly confident he could win this draw — especially against Mike, who'd proven to be more loudmouth than player. The referee wasn't quite ready, though, which gave Charlie a chance to check Mike out. He held his stick with a reverse grip, right hand down near the blade, and bent way over his skates, which were far apart. The blue team's right winger was lined up at the top of the circle, his stick pulled back slightly for a shot.

Charlie drifted into the circle. Mike probably thought he was solid, but in Charlie's opinion he was completely off balance. The grip he used made it easier to draw the puck back, but his right hand was too low, so he didn't have any power, and his legs were so far apart he couldn't move.

The referee blew his whistle. He held the puck out momentarily, and then dropped it between them. Charlie ignored the puck, instead tying up Mike's stick. He struggled to get it free, but Charlie had position. He spun backwards to knock him off the puck, and calmly kicked it back to Scott.

Scott hesitated slightly, and then fired the puck

around the boards to Zachary, who had read the play correctly and was waiting at the hash marks near the boards. Charlie cut across the top of the circle, and Zachary hit him with a pass near the blue line. Charlie took it at top speed and zipped up the right side. He glanced quickly to his left. As expected, his left winger was too slow to be of much help, but out of the corner of his eye, he spotted Nick steaming up the middle.

Charlie carried the puck over centre. Blue's left defenceman had slowed, determined to stand Charlie up at the blue line. Charlie skated towards him, dipping his shoulder, as if to go outside. When the defenceman began to turn that way, Charlie cut inside. In a flash, he was by him. Nick had caught up, so they had a two-on-one. Charlie swerved to the right to open things up, and Nick slowed slightly to give Charlie a passing angle. The goalie was squared up to Charlie, far out of his crease, apparently confident that his defenceman would prevent a pass across.

The defenceman bent down and laid his stick across the ice to make sure Charlie didn't pass. That move decided the matter for Charlie. With a final burst of speed, he cut outside, with the puck on his backhand and charged for the right side of the net. This forced the goalie to commit to the shot, and also convinced the defenceman that Charlie would shoot. He even dropped to the ice, sliding on his side to block it. Just when it seemed Charlie had run out of room, he flicked a backhand over the sprawling defencemen's legs across the top of the crease. The defenceman slid past the net; the goalie was on his knees and out of position, and Nick had an easy tap-in.

The red players roared their approval. Nick pounded the air with his fist and raced over to Charlie.

"That was too beautiful, my man."

He punched Charlie's outstretched glove and whacked his shin pads with his stick. The other red players joined in, punching gloves and congratulating each other. Charlie felt incredibly relieved, as if a great weight had been lifted from his shoulders. At least he'd shown Tremblay that he could play centre.

Since they had scored so quickly, Tremblay left them out, and half a minute later that paid off in another goal. This time Charlie scored on a wraparound, after a smart pass from Scott. It was a buoyant group of players who headed off to the bench at the end of the shift. Charlie was totally stoked, and he could barely wait to get back on the ice. His wish was soon granted, and although they didn't score this time, his line controlled the play, and Charlie almost put in another one with a hard slapshot from the top of the circle.

Ten minutes later, the blue side scored a lucky goal to tie it up. Matt had gained control in red's end and fired the puck to the front of the net, where it hit a defenceman's skate and bounced in. The blue players all held their sticks up high to celebrate, and the players on the bench pounded the boards.

Another few minutes passed and, with the faceoff in red's zone, Tremblay put two fingers in his mouth and let out a whistle. The ref's head jerked around.

"Time out," Tremblay said.

The referee blew his whistle and pointed to the red team's bench.

Tremblay pulled Charlie's line aside, and waved for Nick and Scott to join them. "There's only about a minute left. I'm putting you five out for the last shift. I know it's just a scrimmage, and the score doesn't matter, but I'd rather win than lose. If you get the chance, drive for the net and try to score."

The players nodded and headed to their zone. Charlie noticed Mike's line coming out.

"Hey guys, hold up," Charlie said.

They turned to look at him quizzically.

Tremblay was right — they may as well try to win, scrimmage or not. "I got an idea," he began. "Mike's not the best faceoff man I've ever seen."

"Not according to Mike," Scott quipped.

"I think I can win the draw cleanly to Scott. Nick, you take off and get to the other side of the net and take a pass from Scott. I'll take off up the middle. Nick fires it up to me, and if we're lucky, I'll be wide open . . ."

They were all staring at him. Charlie swallowed hard. It hit him like a ton of bricks. He barely knew these guys, and here he was bossing them around, telling them to pass him the puck. What was he thinking? They must think he was the biggest jerk. Charlie braced himself for a response.

"I'll slap it hard so they can't intercept," Nick said. "It'll either be a breakaway or an icing."

"I can hold their winger up," Zachary said.

"I'll bank the pass of the boards so you'll get it on your forehand," Scott said, tapping Nick's shin pads with his stick.

Charlie didn't say a word as he approached the face-off circle. Were they just being polite, or did they really buy into the plan? He choked up on his stick and leaned forward. At the very least he'd better make good on his bragging and win the draw. Mike was giving some last-second orders to his winger lined up at the top of the circle, so he straightened back up.

"Move over a few feet — to the left," Mike ordered. "Listen up, dude. To the left, and I'll pull it right onto your stick. Get ready to shoot."

The winger moved over a step — not enough to satisfy Mike, however. He skated over and tapped a spot on the ice.

"Right here, dude. I want you to stand right here."

The winger moved over dutifully.

"Let's line up, blue," the ref said gruffly.

"Give me a minute, will ya?" Mike muttered. "Guy doesn't even know where to line up on a faceoff. Pathetic."

Charlie forced himself to relax his shoulders, his eyes fixed on the ref's hand.

The puck dropped!

Crash.

Their sticks smashed together — but not before Charlie had sent the puck spinning back to Scott. Mike barrelled after the puck, leaving Charlie free to head up the middle. He didn't look back, praying all the time that Scott and Nick had carried out the plan. As he crossed the blue line he spun backwards, and lucky he did, because the puck was ten feet away. True to his word, Nick had blasted the pass from behind the net.

He stumbled momentarily to control the puck, but in a few strides he was off on a breakaway, the two defenders caught completely by surprise. In close, he faked to his backhand, waited for the goaltender to drop to his knees, and then pulled the puck to his forehand and tucked it into the corner on the stick side.

Charlie pounded the ice with his stick and grinned widely as his teammates pounded him on the helmet.

"Perfect pass," he yelled in Nick's ear.

"Perfect play," Nick enthused, adding a whack on the back.

Hilton blew his whistle and waved for all the players to join him at centre. Charlie took a knee next to Scott, Zachary and Nick.

"That was great, guys," he said. "I saw a lot of skill and heart out there. Of course, this is the tough part. I really think all of you could contribute, but like I said, we can only register fifteen skaters and two goalies. I'm going to talk with Coach Tremblay for a minute. Head in to the dressing room, and we'll call you out with our decision."

Charlie reviewed the practice in his mind as he undressed. Obviously, the fight was the low point. But hopefully, he'd redeemed himself during the scrimmage. He had the feeling Coach Tremblay was on his side. He was the one who'd moved him to forward. Hilton had been pretty angry, though . . . It wouldn't be long to wait, anyway.

Mike walked into the room and practically threw himself down on the bench beside Charlie. "Totally bogus," he fumed. "Ref drops the puck before I'm ready. Did that the entire game. You gotta admit the ref was totally lame."

Charlie shrugged. What could he say?

"My stick wasn't even down on that last play. You saw it," Mike continued. "And as if the ice time was fair. This team is totally messed. I mean it."

"Tough for everyone," Charlie managed. He began wondering if he would have been better off sitting next to Jake. He looked around for a place to move, but the room was jammed. He had to endure one complaint after another from Mike who ran down Hilton and Tremblay and practically every player.

The door opened and Hilton walked in.

"Dylan, Pudge and Zachary, can I please speak to you in the hall?"

The three players returned a minute later. Charlie was sure Zachary had made it. That Dylan kid was okay too. Pudge was a solid defenceman, and even though he hung out with Jake and his crew, he seemed different from those guys.

The process was repeated, with another group of three. Charlie did his best to look cool when his turn came, along with Scott and Nick's. The two coaches waited in the corridor, a few dressing rooms away.

Hilton's serious expression changed into an expansive smile when they got near. "Congratulations, fellas, we're going to need all three of you for the team."

Scott gave a loud whoop and clapped his hands. "Awesome," he shouted.

Hilton laughed. "Scott and Nick, we'd like you to team up as a defence pair. You played great today, and I think your styles compliment each other. Nick, we like your offensive ability, and we're going to exploit that. Scott is solid defensively, which will let Nick wander a bit more. As for you," he said, turning to Charlie, "we think the move to centre fit your game perfectly, and that's where you're going to stay. How does that sound?"

"It sounds good," Charlie said, still overwhelmed.

Scott was not so subdued. "It sounds better than good, Coach. It sounds totally good!"

"Just one thing," Hilton said, pointing at Scott and Charlie. "I can't have a repetition of the . . . scuffle. Tryouts are over, and I appreciate that it's a stressful experience. I am counting on you to put all bad feelings aside, and work together as a team."

"You can count on me for that," Charlie said earnestly.

"Ancient history," Scott concurred.

"Good to hear that. Now, can you ask Mike, Richard and Jonathon to come next? I think they're in your dressing room." Hilton asked.

As they made their way back, Scott elbowed Charlie and pointed to Nick. "Can you believe I gotta watch this pretty boy prance around the ice every shift, while I do all the hard work?"

"Doesn't solid defensively really mean can't skate?" Nick asked Charlie.

These two were never serious. Why should he be?

"I'm kinda surprised either of you made it, to be honest," he joked.

Scott stopped short, looking as if he'd seen a ghost. "Does Charlie Joyce have a sense of humour?"

"I did not know that," Nick intoned.

"I'm actually extremely funny," Charlie dead-panned. "Many people consider me the life of the party."

"Not sure I wanna go to that party, Joyce," Scott shot back.

"I think Coach Hilton wants to see you next," Charlie told Mike when they got back to the dressing room. "And Jonathon and Richard too."

Zachary caught his eye. He raised his eyebrows. As inconspicuously as possible Charlie flashed a thumbs-up. Zachary winked and went back to changing. Across the room, Jake, Liam and Thomas were staring at him. No way he'd give them the satisfaction of knowing just yet. He turned away and kept his head down.

Hilton came into the room and held up his hand. "Well, that's everyone," he said. "Once more, I'm sorry we can't take you all. For those who didn't make it, best of luck with your club team, and there's always next year. For the rest of you, be prepared to work hard over the next week. We'll practise tomorrow at the same time. The first game is next Friday, so we've got lots of work ahead of us."

Mike plopped himself next to Charlie looking none too happy.

"Bogus freakin' team! Last time I bother with this stupid school. Haven't won the tournament in, like, forever and he picks the worst players."

Charlie had no desire to listen to Mike's tantrum. He dressed quickly in the hope of missing the rest of it. He wasn't so lucky, unfortunately. As he was about to leave, Mike said, "So, like, how can Hilton make cuts after only two tryouts?"

Charlie hoisted his bag over his shoulder and grabbed his stick. "It's tough to do, for sure — like he told us."

Mike peered up at Charlie. "You didn't make it, did you?"

No point lying. "Um, well, sort of."

"What do you mean, sort of?"

"I'll catch you later," he replied, leaving without answering any more of Mike's questions.

As he walked towards the arena doors he spotted a player standing by the window, his back to him. He looked familiar, although from behind he couldn't tell who it was.

"That was a sweet goal," the player said, turning around. Pudge blushed slightly and pushed the door open for Charlie.

"Thanks," Charlie said, stepping into the cool night air.

Charlie couldn't think of anything to say. He nodded, and headed towards home. He'd only taken a few steps when Pudge called out, "So I'll see you at the practice tomorrow."

He whirled around. "How'd you know I made it?" he asked.

"You've got to be kidding. You were the best player out there."

"I don't know about that," he said, "but thanks for the compliment." He paused, then said, "and congrats yourself on making the team."

Pudge gave a mock bow.

As soon as he knew he was out of eyeshot Charlie threw an arm into the air and jumped up. He'd made it. He'd actually made it. That would show Jake and those clowns. Now that he was on the team they'd have no choice but to accept him. Besides, Scott, Nick and Zachary had made it, and they were cool guys. They almost seemed like friends already; and Pudge was making an effort to be nice. So what if Jake and his crew didn't like him? At least there were four guys on the team to hang with. Best strategy was to ignore Jake and just play hockey.

For the first time since coming to Terrence Falls, Charlie was looking forward to the next day.

7

STEPPING UP

It was Wednesday morning, and Charlie was in a situation that was becoming all too common. He had stayed up late finishing his French assignment, and then watched some television before going to bed. The result was a late wake-up and a very slow start to the day. He looked at his watch and groaned. He had ten minutes to drop off his hockey bag at the rink and get to homeroom. He struggled to run, but his bag, slung over his shoulder, made anything more than a quick shuffle impossible. His helmet had somehow lodged itself into the small of his back and was banging on his spine, but he didn't dare stop.

When he turned the corner and the arena came into view, he took off as fast as he could.

"Oh great," he said under his breath.

Jake and Liam were up ahead. He wasn't about to walk with them, so he slowed to a walk, resigning himself to yet another late slip — and probably a stern lecture from Hilton.

"Come on, already," he muttered.

The two boys had stopped. He thought they were talking about something at first, but then he noticed Pudge off to the side. They weren't letting him on the sidewalk, taking turns ramming him with their hockey bags. He heard Jake and Liam laughing, as if they were just having a good time, but the horseplay had a touch of cruelty. He'd seen this before and, in his opinion, Pudge was being bullied. Pudge had gone out of his way recently to help him out, telling him about the school, the other players on the team, and the general gossip that a new kid like him could never know. The sight of him being pushed around by his supposed friends made Charlie's blood boil.

He watched in anger from a distance. That anger turned white hot when Jake kicked Pudge's hockey bag on the side, karate-style, and sent Pudge crashing to the ground. Liam and Jake hooted and hollered, exchanging high-fives. Pudge lay on the ground, looking like he'd had the wind knocked out of him.

Without thinking about what he was doing, Charlie ran to Pudge's side, dropping his bag and stick, and reached out a hand to help him up. Pudge seemed on the verge of tears, but he stifled them back and got up himself.

"What's your problem, Jake?" Charlie said. "What was that all about?"

"Maybe you want some of that too?" Jake snarled.

"Maybe you want to get a life," Charlie said.

His heart pounded in his chest, and he knew that a

fight would mean getting kicked off the team, and maybe even a suspension from school, but he was too mad to care.

Jake stepped towards him, his fists balled. Liam held up his hands. "Cool it, bud. If Hilton hears about this, we're off the team. This isn't smart. Remember what he said to us."

Jake continued to glare at Charlie. "We'll pick this up at a later date, Chuckles," he said, heading off towards the arena.

Liam walked backwards, keeping an eye on Charlie. "You've made your last mistake, punk. We'll take care of you. Count on it. Coach can't protect you forever. Your life's over once the tournament's done." And with that parting shot, he ran to catch up with Jake.

Charlie watched them as they went through the arena doors.

"That wasn't a very good idea. You don't want to get on the wrong side of those guys — especially Jake," Pudge said in a soft voice.

"Too late for that," he said. He was all too aware of the danger Jake represented, but he pretended not to care, and went over to retrieve his bag. They continued on to the arena, neither saying a word. Charlie finally broke the silence by asking a question he'd had on his mind since the first day of school.

"I gotta ask you," he began. "Why do you hang out with those guys?"

Pudge didn't respond at first. Finally he said, "They're not usually that bad. A little worse lately is all."

"I don't think you need to put up with their garbage. You're a big guy, and you can handle any of them."

Pudge cast his eyes down. "I don't know about that — maybe. But I've known them since grade school. I don't have any other friends at school." His voice trailed off.

Charlie could see that Pudge was embarrassed. That made sense since no one wants to admit to being bullied. Best to change the subject. A random idea popped into his head — kind of crazy, but in a way it made perfect sense. Pudge obviously didn't want to talk about Jake, so Charlie figured he may as well ask now.

"I was talking to Zachary yesterday after practice," he said. "You know Zachary, right?"

Pudge nodded.

"Anyway, we kinda got put on the same line, with me at centre and him on right wing." Pudge was looking straight ahead. Was he even listening? "Yeah, anyway, so we've had a couple of guys on left wing. Don't know why, but no one's really worked out." Pudge remained unresponsive. Charlie pulled Pudge's arm and tapped his bag with his stick. "Maybe I could ask Hilton if you could move up and play left wing. You'd be perfect. We need a big, strong winger to get the puck out of the corner — someone to cause havoc in front of the net." He grew more excited as he explained. "You'd also cover up defensively for a goal-suck like me," he laughed.

"You're not a goal suck," Pudge replied. "Not like Jake."

"I could talk to the coach before practice today if you want. I'm sure he'd give it a try."

Pudge wasn't convinced. "I've always been a defenceman, and I made the team as a defenceman. I don't think I've played a shift at forward in my life. Besides, we'd have to move a forward back for me." He shook his head. "I don't think Hilton will go for it."

"At least we can ask," Charlie countered. "We'll tell him we've been practising together for the last few days and worked out a bunch of new plays. Zachary will back us up. He's a good guy. What do you say?"

Pudge remained silent.

"You won't have to play with Thomas anymore."

"Tough to argue against that!"

"Come on, we'd better hustle or we'll be late for homeroom, and Hilton may not even let us practise," Charlie said.

They both broke out into a run and raced off to the arena.

8

A NEW LINEMATE

Charlie held out his hands for the ball. It was phys. ed. class, and his teacher, Mr. Barton, had organized a series of three-on-three basketball games. Charlie, Zachary and Scott formed a team, and they were well on their way to winning their third straight game. The score was 8–0. All they needed was one more basket. Scott delivered the ball to Charlie at the top of the key. Charlie faked left, then with a crossover dribble cut to the right and drove to the basket. Two defenders shifted across to stop him. Charlie jumped up, which got the two defenders off their feet, and shovelled a bounce pass to Zachary, who was charging hard down the left lane. Zachary took the pass and calmly took it to the hoop for an easy layup.

The three teammates congratulated themselves on the win. Charlie was an avid player, and had been selected to play for the city all-star team last year for his age group. He was about to ask where they had learned to play when Mr. Barton blew his whistle.

"We only have about seven minutes left," he bellowed. Mr. Barton had been a phys. ed. instructor at Terrence Falls for more than thirty years, and from what Charlie had been told, in all that time he'd never said anything quietly. "Most of you have finished your matches, so how about a game of dodge ball to end things up?"

The boys responded with an enthusiastic cheer, and bounded around the gym, while Barton went into the equipment room for a ball.

Ms Cummings, followed by thirty grade-nine girls, walked into the gym just as Barton left. They had been outside running track. As Barton emerged from the room with a red rubber ball, Cummings waved and went over to speak to him. This was her first year at Terrence Falls, and she seemed as quiet as Barton was loud. Cummings whispered something to Barton, who in turn looked surprised.

"A capital idea, Ms Cummings Listen up, everyone. The ladies have finished early also. They're going to join in on the dodge ball game."

He turned to Cummings to explain the rules. "It's a simple game. Students can run anywhere in the gym. Whoever has the ball tries to throw it at someone. If you hit someone below the waist, they're out. The thrower's out if someone catches the throw. If you try to catch a throw but drop it, then you're out. You can take three steps with the ball. Bouncing the ball gives you three more steps. Hits above the waist don't count. Hit someone in the head, you're out."

Cummings listened politely. "They've played before," she murmured.

"Tremendous," he shouted. "Then let's go!"

Barton walked to the centre of the gym and pounded the ball into the floor with his fist. The ball bounced high into the air, nearly touching the ceiling, while several of the more adventurous players stood underneath to try to catch it.

Everyone started to yell, some shouting encouragement, others challenges. The action was fast and furious. It was a small gym, and with so many players, people were getting hit with nearly every throw. Before too long, only five remained. Scott and Zachary, who had worked together as a team, were huddled together in one corner. Charlie, who had remained in the background to avoid attracting any attention, was in the opposite corner. Jake had the ball in the middle of the gym. Julia, from Charlie's homeroom, stood under one of the basketball nets.

Jake looked around, and then charged at Scott and Zachary, holding the ball up over his shoulder with his right hand, making as if to throw. Zachary held his ground, but Scott decided to run for it. Jake instantly swerved towards Scott, sprinting behind him, bouncing the ball to gain three more steps. Jake raised his arm again. Scott jumped, anticipating a throw but Jake cleverly held onto the ball. When Scott landed, Jake was three feet away, and all he had to do was toss it lightly off Scott's knee to get him out.

Jake was on the ball like a cat, and soon had Zachary

cornered. He made short work of him, using his favourite move — faking a throw to get him to jump, and hitting him when he landed. That left Julia and Charlie, with Jake still holding the ball. He was at the opposite end of the gym, and was dribbling the ball, moving steadily closer. Charlie was on the verge of running to another corner, when Julia came over and pulled on his sleeve.

"I have an idea," she whispered. "Let's stick together." She waved at Jake. "We'll let you off easy if you just give us the ball," she challenged.

That set the onlookers off.

"So give her the ball, Jake," one kid laughed.

"Quit now, Wilkenson. You got no chance against her."

"Go, Julia, go!" her friends began cheering.

Since that first day of school Charlie hadn't dared speak to Julia. She always hung out with a ton of friends. He had enough problems without being snubbed by a bunch of girls. Even so, he'd noticed her. She was the best girl athlete in grade nine, and judging from her answers in English, she was smart too. He'd always been a bit shy around girls. With everyone watching, and Jake moving towards them, he was completely tongue-tied. A nod was all he could manage.

"Spread out a bit," she said, pushing his shoulder. Charlie moved dutifully over a few feet.

Jake had picked up speed, but then slowed, confused by the odd strategy. Charlie didn't get it either — it didn't make sense to let yourself be cornered. Charlie crouched down low, certain that Jake would go after him. Suddenly, he got it. Julia had tricked him to take the focus away from her. He looked over. She winked. He felt himself flush deeply. Why was he so lame? He totally fell for it. The entire school would be howling about this by lunchtime.

Jake stood still, about ten feet away, holding the ball in his throwing hand, enjoying the attention. All the kids were watching intently. Everyone knew about Jake and Charlie. They too expected him to finish Charlie off.

Without warning, Jake took two large steps and drew his arm back. He had a powerful arm. Charlie figured it'd be impossible to catch the throw, so he decided to try and dodge out of the way and trap the rebound off the wall. He leaned forward on his toes, readying himself. Jake brought his arm forward and Charlie jumped to his right, spinning at the same time.

A huge roar sounded from the class. The ball hadn't touched him. What happened? He looked around frantically for the ball. Jake hadn't moved. He was looking up at the ceiling, his eyes closed. Charlie felt the ball touch his knee.

Julia stood next to him holding the ball in her hand.

"What happened?" he gasped.

"I figured Jake would try to take me out first — you know, cause I'm just a girl. I caught the ball — and now you're out." She raised her eyebrows a few times and grinned.

Jake must have thrown at Julia at the last second.

"How'd you know he'd do that?"

Julia tossed the ball to him. "Jakey's not as clever as he thinks."

A group of girls started chanting.

"Ju-li-a! Ju-li-a! Ju-li-a!"

"Girls rule — boys drool."

As her friends gathered around to congratulate her, Charlie eased himself away, uncomfortable among all those girls. He didn't get away unnoticed, however.

"What do ya think about the new champ, Charlie?" a girl said in a teasing voice.

A few of the girls giggled. Julia elbowed one of her friends.

"Don't let them bug you, Charlie," Julia said. "Most of them are demented anyway."

Charlie was overwhelmed. "I won't," he said with an awkward smile, beating a hasty retreat. He could only imagine what they were saying as he walked over to the storage room to put the ball away.

"Joyce-man. What's the deal-i-o?"

Scott laughed, hands on his hips, with Zachary smirking behind him.

"I didn't see the throw," he stammered.

"Very interesting," Scott replied. "But we were more interested in what you and Julia were talking about."

"What do you mean? When?"

Zachary snorted. "Like right now, after the game. You guys seemed to be having an intense conversation."

"We barely said two words to each other."

"I think she would have said more if she'd had the chance," Scott said.

"Trust me guys," he said. "I'd give you fifty bucks each if she even knows my name."

Scott slapped Charlie on the back. "Fork over the cash, Joyce. She knows your name."

He and Zachary shared a chuckle together, as if they were in on some secret joke. Charlie held up his hands in mock surrender. He was about to respond, then decided to just change the subject by asking them about Pudge.

"I had a great idea," he began. "I found a left winger for Zachary's and my line."

"Sidney Crosby has decided to play for us," Scott joked.

"Not that I know of," Charlie said. "And he's a centre, anyway."

"You can be replaced," Scott said.

"Listen," Charlie said. "I was talking to Pudge before school — and then it hit me."

"Like a thunderbolt," Scott interrupted. He turned to Zachary. "I've heard love hits that way too. Like after a dodge ball game, two people can suddenly fall in love and . . ."

Charlie cut him off. He was in no mood to joke around about him and Julia, not that there was anything to joke around about. "I had an awesome idea — we should ask Hilton to move Pudge up to left wing to play with me and Zachary. We could totally use his size down low in the corners and in front of the net, and since he played defence, he'd be pretty responsible in our own zone."

Zachary shrugged, seemingly unimpressed.

"He's always struck me as a stay-at-home defence type, and not all that good with the puck," Scott said. "I doubt he'd make much of a forward. And, between you and me, I don't think he even deserves to be on the team. He just made it because he's part of Jake's little club, and he's Thomas's defence partner. What's he ever done in practice?"

"I think he's a solid player," Charlie said. "He almost never makes a mistake. He plays the body well, he's rarely out of position, and he's a lot faster than you think. I'm really stoked about the idea — it'll be a good move."

"Zachary, what do you think?" he asked his left winger directly.

Zachary shrugged again. "I guess he couldn't be much worse than what we've been playin' with so far. Can't say I noticed him at the tryouts or the practices. Figured he was part of Jake's crowd, is all. Don't really know the dude. If you think it's a good idea, then whatever." He paused and added, "Although, I gotta tell you, I'm not really stoked about having one of Jake's boys on our line."

"Don't worry about it," Charlie said, more than happy to take that as a yes. "I'll take care of everything."

"You go for it," Scott replied.

Not the most positive response, but at least they hadn't said no. Unfortunately, the big hurdle was still ahead of him — Hilton. He'd have to wait until after school to talk to him. Charlie followed Scott and Zachary into the locker room. Science was his last class of the day, and then they had a practice. He showered and changed as quickly as he could. His teacher had threatened him with a detention if he was late again.

9

SHINNY SHENANIGANS

Practice was scheduled to start in thirty minutes — and Charlie was still waiting by the front doors for Hilton. He must have missed him somehow. Charlie began to jog down the street towards the arena. Not only would he have to tell Pudge that he'd messed up, he'd probably be late for practice. Hilton would love that. He looked back at the school. Nothing seemed to go right.

His luck proved better than he'd thought, however. He spotted Hilton driving out of the parking lot. Charlie spun around and charged back, waving his arms furiously. He breathed a big sigh of relief when Hilton slowed down and pulled over.

The window lowered. "Are you practising today?" Hilton asked. "You're not hurt, are you?"

Charlie shook his head. "I'm fine. I wanted to talk to you about something. I thought you'd come out the front, but I guess you took the side door. Anyway, could I ask you about something before practice?"

Hilton reached over and opened the passenger door.

"Come on in," he said. "We're a bit late, so you may as well come with me. We can discuss whatever's on your mind while we drive."

Charlie got into the car. He felt extremely nervous. He seemed to get that way whenever he was around this man. It was not that he didn't like him — just the opposite. Hilton most definitely knew his hockey — Charlie had already learned a great deal about the game after only a few practices. And he even made English class interesting! He hadn't spent any one-on-one time with him, though, and Charlie always felt uncomfortable with new people.

Hilton started driving, while Charlie desperately tried to think of how to broach the subject. Fortunately, Hilton came to his rescue.

"So what is it you wanted to talk about?" he said.

Charlie took a deep breath and launched into it. "It's no big deal, really. I just wanted to bounce an idea off you, about the team, and about my line."

"I'm listening."

"Zachary and I were thinking about all the left wingers we've been playing with the last few scrimmages. We seem to have cycled through three or four different guys already — a different one every practice, it seems. We're a little worried about it because nothing is working too well. So far nobody seems to play the same game as Zachary and me. I like to get the puck early, and carry it at the defence, then make a quick play to my wingers. Zachary knows exactly what I want, like he knows what I'm about to do almost before I do it. The other guys just don't get it very well. Passes aren't getting to us on time, and everything's disconnected."

Charlie fell silent. This wasn't going well. His coach didn't look impressed. And small wonder! He'd just told him that the other players weren't good enough for him and Zachary. He barely knew the man, had started a brawl at practice, and now was criticizing his teammates! The coach must think he was a total jerk.

Hilton didn't say a word. He just waited for Charlie to continue.

"That didn't really come out the way I wanted," Charlie began. "Let me start over. What I meant to say was that the guys we've played with have all been great. They have lots of skills, good skaters, and good with the puck too . . . I'm having trouble saying it, but, for whatever reason, we haven't played very well together. Have you ever played with certain guys, and the game seems so simple and fun? That's the way it is with Zachary and me. We just click on the ice — and we haven't clicked with the other guys. And I have a feeling you think so too, because you've moved so many wingers on and off our line."

He looked over at Hilton. "Is any of this making sense, or am I sounding like an idiot?"

"You're not sounding like an idiot," Hilton said, looking over at Charlie. "I know what you mean. Some players suit your style, and you can't exactly say why."

He shrugged. "You get on the ice with other players, even guys who are much better, and you never get anything started."

"That's it," Charlie broke in eagerly. "I'm not criticizing the other players. I just know that the team would have an awesome line if we could find a left winger who was more in sync with how we play."

"So you think your line will be awesome?"

He shouldn't have said that. Now it sounded as if he was bragging about how great a player he was. "I'm not saying we'd be the first line. I know Jake, Liam and Matt are the first line," he stammered. "I meant that we would be another strong line. We could take the pressure off Jake, and maybe score a few goals also."

"So you think your line will score a lot of goals?"

Charlie wanted to jump out of the car. If he kept this up, he'd be lucky to be on the team, let alone get Pudge moved to forward.

"No, that's not it. I mean, I hope we do, but I'm not saying we will, like a guarantee or anything. It doesn't really matter who scores, I guess. We just want to win." His voice trailed off. He was lost. He didn't know what to say next.

Again, Hilton helped out. "You were going to ask me about something?"

"That's right."

"Then you'd better hurry, because we're at the rink, and practice starts in about fifteen minutes."

He parked the car and turned to face him.

Charlie decided his best bet was to pretend that the three of them had played together before — the experience factor. He couldn't do worse than he'd done so far, he reasoned.

"Zachary and I were playing together on the weekend, just some shinny — no big thing — and Pudge was there too. We somehow ended up on the same line. I don't know how, because Pudge always plays defence. Before school started I played some pickup at this rink, and Pudge played defence the whole game. Of course, no one plays their position for too long in shinny — I guess you've played a few pickup games in your life?"

Hilton nodded, a slight smile creasing his features.

"So this is the thing. Once we got on the ice together we were practically unstoppable. It was totally bizarre. Pudge never played forward in his life, at least that's what he told me after. And you wouldn't necessarily think of him as a forward. He's a stay-at-home defenceman, always headmanning the puck. I don't think I've even seen him take a rush, or even try to. You should have seen him, though. He was all over the ice. He's got a great shot, and with his size, he's almost impossible to move from in front of the net. He's fantastic in the corners, digging the puck out and centring it to Zachary and me. He must have scored four or five goals, and set me up for another four."

"You were playing shinny on the weekend?" Hilton asked.

"That's right."

"Where?"

Charlie hesitated. What should he say? There was no backing down now.

"We played here," he said.

"What time was the game? I didn't know they had a regular shinny game on the weekend."

"I'm not sure if it's a regular game," Charlie said.

"Okay. What time was the game?"

"I can't remember exactly. I think it was in the morning — early in the morning."

"As in six in the morning?"

"Not that early. It was around eight or nine. I'm not sure, but I think it was around then."

Charlie's mind was reeling. Hilton wasn't buying into the pickup game — that was obvious. Why'd he even say that? All he had to do was come straight out and ask. Lying was the worst thing to do — and to be caught! This idea was headed straight for disaster. In fact, disaster was not going far enough. All he wanted to do was get out of that car and go home.

"We only have six defencemen on the team," Hilton said. "Someone will have to move back. I'm not sure who could do it. I'd have to put some thought into it. If I'm not mistaken, Pudge has played with Thomas for a few years, both with a club team and on the grade-eight school team. I'd hate to split them up."

Charlie was so relieved that he'd stopped asking about the invented pickup game, that he wasn't too disappointed that Hilton didn't like the idea.

"I appreciate that," he said. "No big deal. I just

wanted to ask, that's all. If you don't think it can work, then forget about it."

"I didn't say that. I just need to consider it a bit more. Why don't you leave it with me, and we'll see how it goes.

"Sounds good to me."

"Have you checked this out with Pudge?" he asked sharply.

Charlie was confused. Was he going to actually consider it, even after his ridiculous story about an early morning pickup game? He nodded slowly. "He's all for it. We talked about it. He said he'd always played defence, but would move up if it helped the team. He thought it would be fun, playing forward, that is."

"I was a forward back in my time," Hilton said, "so I can understand that." He laughed. "To be honest, I never could understand defencemen. How can you stay back all the time, waiting for the other team to attack? One mistake, and there's a goal in the net. I could never do it. Too selfish, I guess!"

Charlie laughed also. "You could be talking about me too."

Hilton looked at his watch. "You'd better get a move on," he said. "Practice is in less than ten minutes, and you'll be late if you don't hustle."

"No problem," Charlie said.

He got out of the car and closed the door. After a few steps he stopped, came back, and opened the door.

"Thanks a lot, Coach," he said, closing the door again and running off to the rink. He sprinted through the lobby towards the dressing rooms.

It was a miracle, but he had a feeling that things had somehow worked out. Hilton was certainly an interesting person. You never knew what he was thinking. If he would only give Pudge a try on the wing. Charlie had a feeling that it would only take one practice together to prove themselves.

10

THE VOTE

Charlie barely made it onto the ice before Hilton blew his whistle and waved the players to centre.

"We're going to work on some forechecking and offensive zone coverage today," Hilton announced. "We can scrimmage a bit at the end, if we have time. Coach Tremblay couldn't make it, so bear with me and try to listen. Some of this stuff is a bit technical, but it's important, so let's try to concentrate for the next half an hour."

He held up a large whiteboard with rink markings on it, and invited all the players to kneel down in front of him. "This is how I'd like to pressure the other team on the forecheck. The hockey world calls it the left-wing lock."

"What about the trap?" someone called out.

Hilton shook his head. "I don't like the trap — and certainly not for high-schoolers. We're going to play a more aggressive style. Anyway, listen up. The basic concept is simple. Look here."

He rapidly sketched his forechecking scheme on the board.

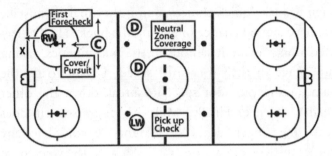

"The X marks the puck, and we're the Os. Assume the puck's been dumped into this corner. The player closest to the puck, the right winger in this case, is the first forechecker and he pressures the puck in deep. The next player, usually the centre, plays up high, around the top of the circle, and moves to where the defenceman is most likely to pass it, usually up the boards or around the net. The two forecheckers take turns pressuring the puck, cycling the zone while the puck flips from side to side. The idea is to pressure the defence into passing early, so we can get a turnover inside the line.

"Meanwhile, the other three players spread out in a line across the ice in the neutral zone. They divide the ice into three equal zones, and each player is responsible for covering that zone, all the way back to his own net. The defencemen line up behind the two forecheckers, with the left winger next to them. It's critical that these three players resist the temptation to go in deep. They must stay in the neutral zone, waiting for a turnover, clogging the middle, and trying to intercept any breakout passes."

Hilton lowered the board and looked at his players. "I like this forechecking style because it forces defence-men to make quick choices, and if they make a mistake we have a good chance of getting the puck. The Detroit Red Wings made it famous in the mid-nineties, taking advantage of their forwards' speed. I want to do the same, using our foot speed to break down the other team's defence. Finally, while it's aggressive, it does leave one winger back. If done right, we won't have any three-on-twos or two-on-ones. We have to avoid those at all costs. So, any questions?"

No one put up a hand.

"Either you guys are absolutely brilliant, or no one understood a word I just said," he laughed. "Let's find out. To start, I want Jake's line up. Give me Nick and Scott on defence. I'll have the puck in the right corner, and we'll go through it a few times, just to work on positioning. Everyone else pile onto the bench, and watch closely. We'll switch it up, so everyone gets a turn." He paused, and added, "Pudge, I want you up with Charlie's line for this. Adam, you move back and play with Thomas." He didn't wait for any reaction, skating off with the puck to start the drill.

Charlie couldn't believe it. Just like that and it was done. He skated over to Pudge.

"You're amazing," Pudge said. "I didn't think he'd even give me a chance."

"You have no idea how amazing this is. I sounded like a total spaz when I asked him. I started telling him about how we played together on the weekend."

"We never played together."

"I know — and I think he knows that too. That's why it's so bizarre. I thought for sure he'd say no. But then as I left he said he'd consider it. I guess he did."

Zachary joined them on the bench. "You're quite the general manager," he said to Charlie, pointing to Pudge. "I didn't know you were such a powerful guy."

"You'd better pass me the puck, or you'll be watching from the press box," Charlie said.

"I've always wanted to sit up there. You can see the whole ice."

Hilton gave his whistle a sharp blow.

"Okay, guys. Line up how I showed you. Jake you move in a bit, and Matt, I want you over closer to the middle. Liam, you come closer to me. Remember, your job is to get me to pass the puck quickly — you don't want me to have the time to get a good look."

For the next thirty minutes the team practised their forechecking. It was a little boring at times, especially since Hilton blew his whistle almost every five seconds to point out mistakes and explain how to do it better. Charlie loved it, though. Hilton had a way of making the most technical aspects of hockey seem simple. It was always fun to learn something new, especially when it made you a better player.

Eventually, Hilton blew his whistle and pointed at centre. "Let's have a scrimmage, and try to forecheck like we've just practised. You all look like you could use some action. Jake and Charlie, your lines will start.

Thomas and Adam, you're on Charlie's team, and Scott and Nick, you're with Jake."

The puck was dropped, and soon they were racing around the ice, forechecking scheme completely forgotten. Hilton reminded them a few times about it, but it didn't seem to have much effect. After a while he gave up and let the players enjoy themselves.

Pudge acquitted himself fairly well in his new position, encouraged by Charlie's incessant praise. He slapped Pudge's shin pads after every shift, and he made a great show of celebrating when Pudge scored a goal. Charlie and he had come down on a two-on-one. Charlie had faked a move outside, and then slid the puck between the defenceman's feet to Pudge, who fired the puck into the top right corner, just over the goalie's blocker.

Charlie was relieved to see that by the end of scrimmage Zachary had accepted Pudge. Pudge's performance seemed to have won him over, because he overheard Zachary explaining some new plays to Pudge, the pair sounding as if they'd been linemates for years.

The sound of the Zamboni firing up announced the end of practice. A few of the more energetic players, Charlie included, took some final laps, enjoying the chance to skate full out. Only the driver honking his horn, combined with two loud whistle blows from Hilton, convinced them to get off.

Hilton followed them to the dressing room. He knocked on the door to get the players' attention. "Gentlemen, before you get changed, we need to take care of some business. It has become a tradition at Terrence Falls to hold an assembly with the entire school before the tournament and announce the members of the hockey teams. Part of that tradition is to name the team captains and assistants. So if we don't want to break with tradition, we need to pick some, and we may as well do it now."

A feeling of tension had entered the room, and the guys looked around nervously at each other.

"I'm going to open the floor to nominations. Please don't just call out a name. Give it some thought. Your captain must be someone you respect both as a player and a person. It doesn't have to be the best player, or the guy who scores the most goals. It's someone you feel you can trust. Someone you want to act as a go-between, between you and me, and also someone you feel comfortable talking to. The second and third runner-ups in the vote will be the assistant captains. And as far as I know, no one's being sentenced to death, so you can all relax."

That broke up the tension, and everyone laughed.

"We'll do it this way. Call out a candidate and I'll write the name down on this board. The vote will be by secret ballot, so don't worry about having to vote in front of everyone." He gave one of the players a cardboard box filled with small slips of paper and a bunch of pens. "Take a pen and one slip of paper before we start."

The players passed the box around. Charlie took his and looked around the room. He didn't know the grade ten players too well. Among them, Ethan Mitchell, a defenceman, seemed like a good guy. Among the grade nines, he guessed Jake had the best chance of being captain. Tough to say about assistants. Matt and Thomas were good players and fairly outgoing. He certainly wasn't a Thomas fan. Matt, on the other hand, hadn't bothered him recently, at least not since their fight. Charlie had even grown to admire his determination and spirit on the ice. Matt was more of a team player than he'd given him credit for.

"It looks like we're all ready," Hilton said. "You've also had a minute or so to consider your choices. Before we start, however, I want to emphasize that this is no big deal. It's not a popularity contest, or any judgement about your hockey skills. If you don't get nominated, or if you get nominated but not chosen, please do not take it personally. Teams need leaders, which is why we're doing this, but every player on the team is important. There'll be no special privileges for the captain or the assistants, I can promise you that." He took a deep breath. "All right! Enough with the preliminaries. Let's have some nominations."

Liam held up his hand first. "I nominate Jake."

Hilton nodded. "Anyone else?"

"I nominate Thomas," Matt called out.

"Can defencemen be captain?" Jake wisecracked.

"I think so," Hilton replied.

"I nominate Ethan," another player said.

"I nominate Craig."

The room went quiet after that. No one seemed willing to put forward another name.

Finally Pudge's hand shot up.

"I nominate Charlie Joyce," he said, in a loud voice. That caught everyone's attention. Jake's face clouded over. He glared menacingly at Pudge.

"Any more nominations?" Hilton asked.

The room was silent. "Okay, the nominations are closed," he said, finally. "List three names in order of preference. The player you want to be captain is number one, and the others are your choice to be assistants."

The players quickly wrote down their choices and dropped the slips of paper back into the cardboard box.

"I'll count these up tonight, and you'll find out in two days at the assembly." Hilton nodded to his players and left the room.

Charlie sat in disbelief. Pudge's nomination shocked and embarrassed him. He saw the other players looking over at him, and then turning away. They were obviously also surprised. He really wished Pudge hadn't done that. It's not that he didn't appreciate it — Pudge was probably just trying to be nice. But it wasn't the kind of attention he needed right now. He undressed as quickly as he could, hoping to get out of there before anyone asked him about the vote. He didn't even bother drying his skates before he zipped his bag, grabbed his sticks and left the dressing room.

Charlie fretted all the way home. He'd been tempted to withdraw his name right then and there, although Hilton might have thought that kind of weird. He slapped his stick on the sidewalk. It had happened so fast. It was over before he knew it. Jake and his friends were going to be ten times worse than usual after this.

He saw his house up ahead. Why did Pudge do that? He felt his anger rise — then, curiously, it went away. He shouldn't blame Pudge. How can you get mad at a guy who nominates you for captain? And besides, he had to admit that deep down it was nice to know that at least one player on the team thought him worthy — and nominating a guy Jake hated was a bold move. He hadn't thought that Pudge had the guts to challenge Jake so openly.

Charlie tossed his equipment into the garage. Obviously, there was no sense worrying about it. Anyway, he had an even more pressing problem — homework! He had enough assignments to sink a ship, and had barely gotten started on any of them.

11

A MEETING OF MINDS

It was the day after the vote, and Charlie still couldn't get it out of his mind. He put his book down and looked out the window for what felt like the hundredth time since he sat down to do his book report. To his surprise he saw a kid on a bike wearing a dark blue sweatshirt turn sharply into his driveway. That was a Terrence Falls sweatshirt, he noticed.

The doorbell rang.

"Someone is here to see you," Danielle yelled.

"Okay. I'll be right there."

Charlie ran downstairs and opened the door. Pudge waved a Frisbee.

"Wondered if you wanted to toss the bean around at school before dinner?" He paused. "Are you doin' anything now?"

"I'm workin' on my book report."

"Cool. I just finished mine."

"I'm jealous. I just started. It took me an hour to come up with a title. I can't seem to get started. Not sure if Hilton's gonna be impressed with five blank pages."

"What are you doing it on?"

"I chose *Animal Farm*."

"Any good?"

"Actually, it is. I was surprised. I was up half the night finishing. It got pretty exciting at the end."

"What's it about?

"Animals take over a farm."

"How do they do that?"

"The animals can talk to each other. The farmer is this cruel nutbar — and they chase him off. Then the animals start turning on each other. It's kinda complicated — very intense stuff."

"When you're done with it maybe I'll read it. Sounds kinda interesting."

Charlie leaned against the door. "Yeah, okay. No problem. I'll bring it to school tomorrow."

"So do you need a break from all that heavy thinking?"

"I don't think so. I've barely done any thinking at all."

Pudge's face fell. "That's cool. I understand you wanna get it done."

Charlie knew he should keep working. It was due first thing Monday morning. Frisbee was tempting, though. And it would be rude to say no. Maybe a game of Frisbee was what he needed to get the creative juices flowing.

"Let's do it. No point staring at the wall any longer.

I'll finish it after supper. Hold on while I get my shoes."

Pudge grinned. "Awesome. I'll wait for you on the road." He hopped on his bike and rolled down the driveway.

Charlie went into the living room. His grandmother and sister were reading together on the sofa.

"Grandma, I'm just going out with a friend for a bit."

"Who's the friend?"

"A guy from school."

"Okay, dear. Your mother will be back from work soon. She said we're eating at six-thirty, so don't be too long."

"I won't."

"Have fun," she said, resuming her reading.

Charlie put on his running shoes, grabbed his bike from the garage, and joined Pudge.

"I hope I didn't surprise you too much yesterday . . . after practice, with the nomination," Pudge said as they pushed off. "You got dressed pretty fast. I got the feeling that maybe you weren't too happy about it."

Charlie shrugged. "I admit I was surprised. You didn't have to do that, though. I don't know many guys on the team, so . . ." His voice trailed off.

"I wasn't doing it as a favour. I really think you'd make the best captain — and I think you have a good chance of winning."

"Ethan will be captain, or maybe Jake," Charlie replied.

"Maybe. I'm not sure about Jake. He's been a real

jerk lately, even by his standards, and I don't believe he has as many friends as he thinks."

"It doesn't matter," Charlie replied uneasily. He'd never considered the possibility that a grade ten or Jake wouldn't win.

In a couple of minutes they were there. Charlie put his bike down and took off down the field.

"I'm open — hit me, dude," he called out.

Pudge got off his bike and flung the Frisbee — a perfect strike. Charlie barely had to break stride. He whirled and fired it back. Pudge bounced the hovering Frisbee off his fingertips a few times before hauling it in. The guy could obviously play. Charlie was impressed. They settled down into an easy rhythm, challenging each other with longer and longer throws. It was still warm, and it didn't take too long to work up a sweat, as they ran all over the field. After ten minutes or so, Charlie let loose a wild toss, which curved sharply towards the school and crashed into some concrete steps.

Pudge pretended not to see the Frisbee. He held his hand over his eyes, peering all around him. Charlie laughed and jogged over. It was resting against the bottom of the railing. As he leaned down to get it, he heard the familiar sound of a skateboard rolling along the pavement. He looked up in time to see a guy doing a railslide, heading straight for his head. He dropped to the pavement as the boarder flew over him.

The boarder landed easily, threw in an ollie, and then added a 5-0 grind, bringing himself to a full stop.

Incensed at the rider's recklessness, Charlie leapt to his feet, ready to confront him. He took two steps towards him and then stopped short — it was Zachary.

"Hey, dude, how many times do I have to tell you to keep your head up?" he said.

Charlie had to laugh. "A half-second warning is all I'm asking, then you can try to kill yourself on your board."

"Sometimes you just need to let it fly."

They came together and punched fists.

"Nice board," Charlie said.

"Relatively new purchase — a combination Christmas present and forced savings. I just got it before school. Check it out."

Charlie took the board from him. "Do you like the small wheels?"

"I think they're 42 or 43 — and hard as granite. The rating is something like 98."

Charlie was impressed. "I've never been on a board like this."

"I really shouldn't use it on the street. I felt like a quick ride before dinner, and lent my other board to a buddy. I figured, what's the worst that could happen?"

"You could put the nose through Charlie's head!" Pudge said.

He had come over to join them.

"How's it going, Pudge?" Zachary said.

"Good. Tossing the bean around with Charlie." He noticed the new skateboard. "Cool machine," he said. "Check out that deck."

The deck had a bright orange and red sun, with fluorescent flames radiating in all directions.

"Custom job, dudes. A buddy of mine does them."

"Who's that?" Pudge asked.

"You know Griffin Page?"

"I think so. He hangs out at the skate park, right?"

"Hangs out? The guy lives there. You should see him ride. The other day he came flying down a ramp, at maximum velocity, doing a tail powerslide, then after landing he right away cracks off a 360 kickflip, followed by a cab jump, and shuts it down with a nose stall — and I'm talking about within five feet of each other. The guy is a wizard. His vert ramp is totally insane. Gravity has no impact on that dude."

Charlie was about to ask for a translation, but held off. He didn't want to sound like a novice. He'd always considered himself a fairly decent rider — he and his friends used to fool around with their boards at recess. He obviously didn't compare to Zachary, or his friend.

Pudge didn't hesitate to ask, however. "How come you stop speaking English whenever the subject of skateboarding comes up? What's a 360 kickflip? And how do you jump over a cab?"

Zachary gave Pudge a good-natured shove. "Sorry, I forgot I was hanging out with a hockey crowd. The 360 is a combination shuvit and kickflip, so you jump up and spin the board around completely. Cab jump is doing a rotation, fakie, and landing forwards. Named after Steve Caballero. Nose stall is popping up on the nose and grinding it along the ground."

"So what's fakie?" Pudge asked.

"When you do a trick with your weaker foot forward. It's just harder, that's all. Hey, you guys need to come with me to the park and learn some tricks. I can't play with guys with pathetic ollies."

Pudge started waving his hand towards the school. "Hey guys. Where you off to?" he shouted.

Charlie looked up and saw Scott and Nick riding their bikes towards them.

"You guys must love school," Scott said. "Did you ever leave, or are ya waiting to get into the library early?"

"We were going over some math formulas, and reviewing our book reports," Charlie said.

"You need to calm down, Joyce. I don't know what you did in your old hometown, but that's a little too wild for these parts," Scott said.

"So where are you guys off to?" Pudge asked.

"We're going home," Nick said. "We just went to check out the new hockey equipment at Dunn's."

"What's Dunn's?" Charlie said.

"Sporting goods store," Nick said. "They've got all the hockey stuff you need. I had my hands on this Easton — sells for $425, and you can pick it up with your baby finger, it's so light."

"Better yet," Scott said, "I tried on a pair of Mission skates — I think they go for over $700. The sales guy was telling me all about them. Said they have so much support you can carve on a dime. And there's a flex system that adds power to your stride. Apparently, my entire game would change with those things on my feet."

"So Scott offers the guy fifty bucks for them," Nick broke in.

Scott laughed. "You should have been there. He thought I was serious. I kept saying, 'Look, take the fifty, and we'll call it even.' And he kept saying, 'That wouldn't even pay for the laces.' Finally, he figured we weren't going to buy anything, and he told us to leave. I should have bought the laces — those were nice laces."

"Maybe you should have bought one, and then saved up for the other," Charlie said.

"I couldn't afford the box. Forget about one lace," he said.

"Hey, listen to this," Pudge said. "I was working at my Dad's restaurant last night, when a big group of people came in. I recognized a few kids from Chelsea. They were all talking about their big school rally — I guess they do the same thing as us, announce the teams in front of all the students and hand out sweaters. Anyway, according to them, the coaches and players were just trashing Terrence Falls. They even dressed up a dummy with our sweater. It held a sign that read: *Terrence Falls Down*."

"Real funny crew they got there," Scott muttered.

"It would be amazing to beat those guys," Pudge said. "They're so full of themselves."

"Chelsea's gonna be really tough to beat," Zachary said, rolling his board back and forth with his foot.

"Their team is stacked. We've got some talent, but we won't beat them with skill. It'll have to be a total team effort."

"We'll just have to get ourselves a total team," Scott said.

"If you just get those skates," Zachary said, "it'll be a done deal. You can carve circles around everyone."

"I'll have you know that I once actually scored a goal."

"You scored a goal in a game?" Nick exclaimed in mock amazement.

"Okay, it was air hockey, but it still counts."

Charlie laughed along with the others at Scott's joke, but he was nervous about the conversation turning to hockey. He didn't want them talking about the vote.

As if on cue, however, that's exactly what happened.

"What do you think your chances are, Charlie?" Zachary asked.

"What do you mean?"

"I mean, being captain!"

Charlie tried to downplay the entire thing. With a shrug, he said, "I honestly haven't thought about it. Been too busy. I've got this book report for Hilton I've got to do tonight — and last night I had to read the book. Jake might be it."

"I hope not," Nick said. "I don't want to play on a team with him as captain. It's bad enough to be on a team with him at all."

"He already thinks he's captain," Scott said. "I bet

he went out and bought himself a shiny red C for his sweater."

"Where do you buy a C?" Nick asked.

"At the C store," Scott wisecracked.

"I think Charlie's got a real shot at winning," Pudge said, seriously. "A lot of guys feel the same way. Ethan and Craig are good guys, but maybe not skilled enough to be captain. I bet Matt, Liam and Thomas voted for Jake, and that's it."

"Charlie's got five votes right here," Scott said.

"That's not necessarily true," Charlie said.

"Actually, it is," Zachary said. "We all voted for you."

Charlie felt embarrassed. At a loss for words, he finally managed, "I didn't vote for me, so that's four at the most."

They stared at him in disbelief.

"Who'd you vote for?" Scott demanded.

"I believe it was a secret ballot," Charlie said weakly.

"Cough it up," Scott said.

"I voted for Ethan."

They all groaned.

"We'll find out tomorrow, so there's no point worrying about it now," Charlie said, trying to put an end to the discussion.

"I should get going," Pudge said. "Good luck with the report tonight, Charlie, and thanks for the game. I'll see you all tomorrow." He waved to the guys and headed up the stairs.

"I gotta fly also," Zachary said. "I'm getting hungry, anyway. I'll catch up with you dudes later."

Scott and Nick picked their bikes up.

"I hope you realize," Scott said, "that we're racing back to my place, and the loser, who will be you, must say to the victor, who will be me, 'You are the greatest bike racer I've ever seen.'"

"I noticed you've taken the training wheels off your bike," Nick replied.

"I haven't needed them for two weeks now," he said proudly.

"Start us off, Charlie," Nick said.

Charlie nodded and held up his arm. "Gentlemen, start your engines."

Scott made the sound of a revving motor.

"On your marks, get set, go!"

Charlie watched them tear off down the path and over to the road. He followed slowly, as he went to get his bike, thinking about what had been said. He'd been captain of almost every team he'd played on. He'd become used to wearing the C, so it wasn't the responsibility he was afraid of. He had always tried to use his position to make the team better. He remembered his father telling him that the captain's job was to give everyone else the credit when the team won. That advice had always worked, and being captain had been fun. He didn't see much chance for fun if he was named captain of the Terrence Falls team, though. All he saw was a massive headache with Jake, and grade tens wondering why a younger kid was captain.

He rested his bike against the side of the house and pushed open the front door.

"We're in here," his mother called from the kitchen.

Charlie walked in and headed to the sink to wash his hands. His family had already started dinner.

"Grandma tells me you met a friend this afternoon?" his mom said.

Charlie sat down. "We tossed the Frisbee around a bit."

"You also told her that you'd be home by six."

"Sorry, Mom. I lost track of time."

"You lost track of a lot of time — it's after seven! I was beginning to get worried."

"Sorry," he said again.

"I assume you finished your book report."

Charlie flushed. "Not exactly. I have a little more to do on it."

"It's due on Monday, right?"

He nodded. "I was going to try to finish it after dinner . . . and I have tomorrow to work on it."

"I was in your room to tidy up before dinner, and I saw your report on your desk. It didn't look as if you had only a little to finish. It looked as if you had the entire report to do — almost as if you hadn't even started writing?"

"Maybe I haven't written a lot. But I know what I wanna write about . . . sorta."

"And you thought a game of Frisbee was a good idea in that situation?"

"I guess it wasn't such a good idea now that I think about it. I'm going to get started on it right after we eat, I promise."

He could tell his mother was angry. She was strict about school — his father had been too. They demanded good marks, and insisted that he get his work done on time. He knew he was in for it.

"I'm not happy about this, Charles. But why don't you clean up and I'll get dinner for you."

Charlie was more than willing to let it go. He washed his hands, and then started to heap a massive pile of food on his plate. The Frisbee game may not have been a good idea, but he'd sure worked up an appetite.

He listened to his mom and grandmother discuss the café, which was due to open in two weeks. His mother had just hired a waiter and an assistant baker.

"I had to interview about a dozen people," his mother said. "You wouldn't believe some of them. They'd never baked professionally a day in their lives. Most just thought it would be fun. I doubt they could even roll out a pie crust."

"But you eventually found someone?" his grandmother asked.

"A fantastic person. Shirley Goodman is her name. Lots of experience and a really nice personality — I think we'll get along well. She's also new in town, and seemed thrilled to get the job."

"I'm finished," Danielle declared. "Can I watch the rest of my movie?"

"Did you finish your homework?"

"Did it at school."

"All right. Just clear your plate and toss it into the dishwasher."

Once Danielle had left the kitchen, his mother looked over at Charlie.

"I've told you before, that there are some things we like to do, and some things we have to do. School falls under the second category — it is not a hobby. It's important that you keep up with your work, and do your best. I don't care about the marks. I care about the effort. Staying up past your bedtime because you haven't been doing your work on a regular basis is not acceptable. I know you were up late last night reading, and you're probably going to be up late again finishing that report. This has to stop. And if hockey is going to get in the way of school, then there won't be any hockey. Do you understand that?"

Charlie nodded. No point trying to defend himself. He shouldn't have left the report to the last minute, and he never should have agreed to play Frisbee with Pudge. "You're right. I'm having a bit of trouble organizing my time. Hockey's not getting in the way. It's only right now, with the tournament coming up. I'm gonna really buckle down from now on. I promise."

"That sounds good to me," she said.

"Do you mind if I finish my dinner upstairs? I'd like to get started right away."

"Okay. Just remember to bring your plate back as soon as you're done, because I want to run the dishwasher."

"Thanks, Mom."

Charlie gathered his food in one hand and drink in the other, and went to his room. He looked at the empty page on his desk and then over at the clock. He felt depressed. Another late night ahead of him — and tomorrow the assembly, where he'd find out who won the vote.

12

THE RALLY

The girls' and boys' hockey teams sat together on the stage at the end of the cafeteria, which doubled as an auditorium. The room was abuzz with conversation as the entire school crowded in for the assembly. Groups of students huddled in the aisles gossiping and joking around, while just as many others wandered around looking for friends to sit beside.

Principal Holmes tapped the microphone with his finger. "Can everyone take his or her seat — and quickly please," he ordered.

The students ignored him and carried on with their conversations.

"People, I really need your attention. We need to commence the activities immediately."

He got the same reaction the second time. He was about to try again when Hilton came over, leaned over to the microphone, and said, "The sooner we get started, the sooner it's over, so let's everyone sit down and be quiet."

That did the trick. Almost by magic seats were found and talking ceased.

Principal Holmes cleared his throat, and the sound echoed loudly. "Everyone knows why we're here today. It's hockey time! And we've got four terrific teams ready to play this year. I have high hopes for our greatest success yet. The other teams are in big trouble, that's for sure. And you know what I think? I think Terrence Falls is going to win in every division this year, that's what I think." He stopped and nodded his head. No one uttered a sound. The entire student body was silent. Principal Holmes stared out at the students, somewhat bewildered.

He coughed into the microphone, and in a more subdued tone said, "Without further ado, I'd like to call on the coaches to announce their teams. We'll start with the junior girls' team, coached by our new phys. ed. instructor, Ms Cummings."

Cummings came to the microphone, wearing black track pants and a blue sweatshirt with *Terrence Falls* on the front. She called out the names of her players, and then announced that Julia was the captain.

A loud cheer went up, and Julia waved to the crowd before she put on her hockey sweater.

"Hey look," Scott said to Charlie. "Your girlfriend's captain, just like you."

"Scott!" he hissed. "Don't say that . . . the vote's not . . . I mean . . ."

"He's still in denial — about Julia *and* about being captain," Nick stated gravely.

Charlie rolled his eyes and turned his attention back

to the podium. Cummings began to announce the senior girls' team. Scott took some ribbing from his teammates when his sister was announced as captain.

"It's not fair that all the hockey talent went to the oldest child," Nick said.

"It's not fair that I don't have a chance to display my talent on the ice because I have to be your defence partner," Scott shot back.

Charlie interrupted their banter. "I think it's our turn now," he said.

Hilton had taken his place behind the microphone. "Let's have a nice round of applause for the junior and senior girls' teams," he asked. The students obliged with a lusty cheer. The girls returned to their chairs, except Julia and Scott's sister, who were instructed to stand to the side of the stage.

Hilton began to introduce the junior boys' team. One by one the players were called, until the five nominated players remained. Then Thomas and Craig were called. This was the deciding moment. Charlie felt his chest get tight and a flush rise to his cheeks.

Jake and Ethan tried to look cool, but he could see that they were also nervous.

"Now for the names of the two assistant captains and captain," Hilton said dramatically. "One assistant captain will be Ethan Mitchell."

The crowd cheered for Ethan as he went to get his sweater. It was down to Charlie and Jake. The entire school was dead quiet as they waited for Hilton to make the announcement.

Hilton paused once more, and then announced, "The second assistant captain will be . . . Jake Wilkenson."

Charlie felt as if he'd been run over by a truck. Apparently, Jake couldn't believe it either. He snatched his sweater from Hilton and stomped off to stand next to Thomas and Liam. Charlie knew Scott, Nick, Zachary and Pudge had voted for him. Incredibly, enough of the other guys voted for him too. He waited to be announced.

"I give you the captain of the junior boys' team: Charlie Joyce."

Charlie kept his head down as he crossed the stage. He noticed that most of his teammates clapped. He also got a nice round of applause from the audience, which he appreciated because few of them knew him by name. Hilton shook his hand and gave Charlie his sweater. He eagerly put it on. Hilton directed Charlie towards where Julia and Scott's sister were standing, and returned to the microphone.

"Now I'm going to hand the podium over to Mr. Hughes, the coach of the senior boys' team."

Charlie looked over at his teammates. Scott gave him a big thumbs-up, and Zachary nodded approvingly. Then Mr. Hughes began to speak, so Charlie turned to look at him.

"Congratulations, Charlie," Julia said quietly. Her voice surprised him. Somehow he'd forgotten that he was standing next to her.

"Thanks. Same to you."

Scott's sister leaned over and said, "Congrats from

me too. Scottie's told me all about you. Says you're the best player on the team, and a nice guy to boot." She leaned even closer, and added in a whisper, "and I'm glad Jake isn't captain."

Charlie didn't know what to say. Julia didn't say anything either, although it seemed like she was trying not to laugh.

Hilton came up behind the three captains, and said, "Let's keep the conversation to a minimum, so the crowd can hear Mr. Hughes, okay?"

All three of them nodded guiltily, and stared straight ahead as the rest of the team was called out.

Finally, it was all over except for the naming of the captain. This time it was no surprise. Everyone seemed to know that it would be Karl Schneider. The students cheered wildly when he came forward for his sweater. He smiled at the crowd and waved gallantly. Karl was over six feet, and weighed close to 190 pounds. His tight T-shirt displayed his ample muscles. Pudge had told Charlie all about the school's resident superstar. He'd set numerous scoring records through the years, including the most goals for the high school tournament last year. Karl also played junior hockey, and the seventeen-year old was widely expected to be a first round pick in the NHL draft when he was eligible next year.

"Perhaps a few words," Hughes invited.

Karl nodded graciously. He took the microphone out of the holder and walked to the front of the stage.

"Last year," he began, "only one team, the senior boys, got to the finals — Chelsea beat us."

A few students booed loudly.

"But that was last year," Karl shouted.

Everyone in the cafeteria shouted back, and soon they were all chanting, "Ter-rence Falls! Ter-rence Falls!"

Karl held his hand up and things quieted down.

"That was last year, and let me tell you, every Terrence Falls team has gotten better. I've seen the practices, and things are really looking up. I am going to make a prediction, and some may think I'm crazy, but I predict that Terrence Falls will win four gold medals at the tournament. In fact, I guarantee it. Four gold medals!"

Karl held up his right hand, four fingers extended. The students did the same, chanting "Ter-rence Falls!" over and over.

"Starting tonight," he shouted, as if straining to be heard over the crowd, "we are going to start kickin' some serious butt. And the butt we're going to kick most seriously is Chelsea's."

That got an even bigger reaction, and the students got to their feet and cheered Karl on. "I'm proud to be wearing this sweater. And I'm going to be proud of all our teams when the tournament's over."

Karl punched the air with his four fingers still extended, then went over and shook hands with the other captains. Charlie was amazed at the size and strength of Karl's hand, and he held on for dear life as the powerful boy pumped his arm vigorously.

Karl stopped for a moment and said to Charlie,

"I've seen you play, kid. Good luck and don't make me a liar. Win that gold."

Principal Holmes took the microphone back from Karl and was telling everyone that regular classes would start in ten minutes. People began milling around the seats talking excitedly.

"So when do you play your first game?"

Julia was looking up at Charlie, catching him by surprise for the second time. It took a moment for the question to register.

"We play at eight o'clock tonight, I think. I can't remember exactly who we play, but we play at eight."

He tried to think of something else to say, but nothing came to mind. He was beginning to feel foolish when Julia said, "We play before you, then."

"I'll come early to check it out," he replied. "Who do you play?"

"I can't remember either," she said. "Terrific captains we are, eh?"

"I guess we'd better figure that out by second period or people will begin to talk," he said.

"Hey, Julia," a high-pitched voice called out. "Come over here for a sec."

A group of her friends had gathered at the bottom of the stairs.

She took a few steps towards them, then turned back to Charlie. "Lead your team to gold, or Sir Karl will be very disappointed," she said, before heading off to join her friends.

"I'll do my best," Charlie replied.

Scott came up behind Charlie and put him in a headlock, adding a few knuckle rubs for good measure before letting him go. Nick, Zachary and Pudge came over as well.

"I want you to know that it was my vote that put you over the hump, so you have to be nice to me," Scott joked.

"I think it was the fifty bucks I gave everyone," Nick added.

The boys laughed, except for Pudge. In a serious tone, he said, "You deserve to be captain. A lot of the guys told me they voted for you."

"Thanks, Pudge," he said. "I hope I won't let you guys down."

"You'd better not let us down," Scott said. "We made you, and we can break you."

"You got that right," Jake growled as he walked past, followed by Liam and Thomas.

Charlie and his friends watched as they left the cafeteria.

"It never ceases to amaze me what a jerk he is," Scott declared.

Charlie sighed. "I wish I knew why he hates me so much."

"Jake has to be the best player," Pudge said. "I've been on his team since Atom, and he's always been like that. He knows you're better, and he can't handle it."

"We need Jake," Charlie said, deflecting the praise. "He's the best goal scorer we've got, and Liam, Matt and Thomas are no slouches either."

Scott looked startled. He held out his hands to interrupt. "Wait a second," he said. "I thought Charlie was our best goal scorer. That's why I voted for him."

"My specialty is defence, you know that," Charlie replied.

They all laughed. "I'll introduce you to our end sometime, Mr. Defensive Specialist," Nick said.

Principal Holmes clucked disapprovingly. "Boys, please. You're going to be late for class. You simply must get going."

"Coach Hilton asked us to stay behind," Scott replied, "to go over strategy for the game tonight. He wants us to use the four-star abracadabra defensive forecheck lock down."

Nick covered his mouth with his hand and the others struggled not to laugh. Charlie suddenly realized that Scott was joking. The guy had no fear when it came to being funny.

Principal Holmes shook his head. "Dear me. I'll never understand all these sports terms. It's like another language."

Ms Cummings gestured for him from the cafeteria floor.

"Yes, I'm coming," Principal Holmes said. "Please excuse me, boys. Good luck tonight, and I hope the four-star abracadabra . . . locking strategy thing works out."

As soon as he was out of earshot all five boys roared with laughter.

"You're gonna get us suspended one day," Nick

125

said, slapping Scott on the back. "Forecheck lock down — now that's a classic."

"I'm proud of that one myself," Scott said, patting himself on the back.

"We probably should get to class," Pudge said.

They jumped off the stage. Charlie looked back before he left the cafeteria. He wanted to hold on to this moment for a little longer — to be elected captain, in grade nine, was a huge honour. It could also add a huge amount of pressure. All eyes would be on him tonight. He closed the door gingerly and followed the others down the hall to his locker.

* * *

Later that day Charlie sat at the dinner table with his sister and mother. They were eating pasta, a pre-game ritual his father had always insisted on.

His mother had gone to great lengths to make it exactly the way he liked, but Charlie was barely eating, just picking at it with his fork and playing with the sauce.

"You should eat a little something before the game," his mother said.

Charlie shrugged. "I'm not that hungry, I guess."

"Are we perhaps a little nervous?"

"Maybe a little," he admitted. "I just wish that the guys hadn't made me captain. It's not that I don't appreciate it. But I'm new to the team, and it probably would have been better to choose one of the guys who's been around longer."

"I'm sure they voted for you because they liked how

you play and wanted you as their captain."

Charlie was not ready to accept that. "I think they were voting against someone, rather than for me. And I think some of them are going to have second thoughts."

"What do you mean?"

He shrugged and poked at his food with his fork.

"He means they voted against Jake Wilkenson because he's such a jerk," Danielle said.

"Danielle!" Charlie hissed.

"Well, it's the truth," Danielle huffed, sticking her tongue out at him. "Hannah told me, and her sister goes to your school."

His mother put her fork down. "So what's the deal with this Jake Wilkenson?"

Charlie sighed. "I don't really know. We got off on the wrong foot the first day of school. Actually, we got off on the wrong foot even before that, at that pickup game you dragged me to."

His mother gave him a stern look.

"Sorry. The pickup game you took me to. Anyway, he's had it in for me since then. We even had a bit of an . . . argument . . . at one of the tryouts."

"Hannah told me all about it," Danielle said breathlessly. "Charlie nailed some guy during a drill, and Jake and his buddy charged at Charlie. Then another guy pulled another guy off Charlie, and the coaches had to pull everyone apart."

"Thank you, Danielle," their mother said. "It's amazing how you seem to know everything that's going on."

Danielle winked and stuffed a big fork full of pasta into her mouth.

"Now what was this about a fight?" his mom asked.

Just then the doorbell rang.

"I'll get it," Charlie said, relieved not to have to answer his mom. He opened the door. It was Pudge. A car idled in the driveway with the lights on.

"Hey, Pudge. What's up? You off to the game already?"

"My dad wants to see the junior girls play, so we're going early. You wanna come?"

"That would be cool. But my grandparents are coming over. I should wait for them. We'll be leaving soon."

"No problem. I'll see you there."

Honk.

"Okay, Dad. One second," Pudge said between cupped hands. He leaned forward. "I also just heard some news, and I thought you'd be interested.

"You got my attention. What's the news?" Charlie asked.

"Jake, Thomas and Liam went to Hilton to complain about you being named captain."

"That's great!" Charlie groaned.

"They told him it was stupid to make you captain when you didn't know any of the guys. Liam said that Jake had been captain of his school team last year, and it won the district championship, and since some of the same guys are on this team he should be captain."

"So what did Hilton say?" Charlie asked.

"My source suggests that he turned them down flat. He said you won the vote, so there wasn't anything he could do about it."

"How do you know about all this?"

"Jake was doing his usual big-mouth routine after school, and Dylan was there — you know him, he's a forward on the third line. He told me." Pudge looked down the street. "I think he lives around here, actually."

Charlie considered the news. "Thanks for telling me, Pudge. I appreciate it. Maybe they'll drop it now that Hilton's turned them down."

"I doubt it," Pudge said. "Those guys don't let up that easy. I'm a little worried about the game tonight. What do you think they'll do?"

"Hopefully, just play well," Charlie said. "Deep down, those guys want to win as much as you or me. Besides, it's just a weekend tournament. It doesn't really matter who the captain is. We only play six games at the most."

"You could be right."

He didn't sound convinced.

Honk.

"I'd better split. I'll see you at the rink."

"Sure. Sounds good. I'll see ya — and thanks for the info. I owe ya one."

Pudge waved and got into the car.

"Who was that?"

His mom had joined him on the porch.

"That was Pudge. He asked if I wanted to go early. Told him Grandma and Grandpa were coming so . . ."

"That was nice of him. You two starting to become friends?"

Charlie was embarrassed. "I dunno. Maybe, I guess. He's an okay guy. Don't really know him."

"Well, Grandma and Grandpa will be here any minute, so eat up and get ready."

Charlie went back to the kitchen. Pudge's news hardly helped his appetite. He managed one more mouthful and then got ready. By the time they arrived at the arena, his stomach was all in knots. He tried to force the butterflies to calm down, without success.

His mother turned around in the car. "Just have fun out there, dear, and good luck."

"What about me?" Danielle piped up.

"You can have fun too, dear."

"I'd have more fun with a bag of popcorn and a drink."

"I think I can arrange that."

Charlie got out and pulled his bag from the trunk. Fun was the farthest thing from his mind. At least their first game was against Cliffcrest High — according to Pudge the worst team in the tournament. Jake would score a bunch of goals, and he'd be happy. A win was just what the team needed. Then they could get ready for the tough games tomorrow.

13

DEBUT DISASTER

A knock on the door woke Charlie from a restless sleep. Although he'd gone to bed early, he still felt tired, and he moaned loudly as the light shone in through his curtains and hit his eyes. He flopped over onto his stomach and covered his head with his pillow. The memory of last night's game returned to him, for maybe the hundredth time since he'd first tried to get to sleep. He couldn't get it out of his head, and had barely slept all night because of it.

What a disaster. They'd been so confident. Some of the guys were betting on how many goals they'd score. Last year Terrence Falls had beaten Cliffcrest 14–0. Yet, somehow this year they'd lost 4–3. Jake scored all three goals, but still it wasn't enough. Charlie's line played terribly. They'd been on the ice for three goals against, including a giveaway by Charlie in his own end that led to the fourth goal — the winning goal, as it turned out. Charlie's game had been awful, and more than a few of his teammates commented on it, during the game and afterwards in the dressing room.

If Terrence Falls lost one more game they'd be eliminated from the playoff round. So much for the four gold medals. He smashed his fist down on the mattress. His punch didn't make him feel better, and he almost clipped his mother who had come in to make sure he was awake.

Charlie peered sheepishly out from under his pillow. "Sorry, Mom," he said. "I didn't know you were there."

She sat down on the edge of the bed. "Good to know that you were only trying to beat up your bed, and not me."

Charlie turned onto his back. "It didn't give me a very good night's sleep, so I thought I'd teach it a lesson."

"Did it learn?"

"Mattresses are not good students, as it turns out."

She ruffled Charlie's hair. "You weren't much in the mood to talk last night," she said. "Maybe now you can tell me what went wrong during the game."

Charlie sat up, shaking his head. "I wish I knew. It was like I'd never played a game in my life. Everything I did was wrong. I singlehandedly let Cliffcrest win."

"That's going a bit far."

"No, it's not. I was on the ice for almost all of their goals, and I barely had a shot on net. My stupidity gave them the winning goal. Cliffcrest is terrible, and we lost to them." He stopped, too upset to continue.

"I admit it wasn't the best game I've seen you play."

Charlie hung his head. "I can only imagine what the guys think. They vote me captain and I turn in a stinker like that — and in my first game."

"I'm no hockey player, but I know the real Charlie Joyce wasn't playing last night. That was an imposter who stole your sweater. You figure out how to get your sweater back." She ruffled his hair again and left.

Charlie didn't really need to figure out what went wrong. He'd known even before the game ended. Passing when he should have shot, chasing the puck rather than playing his position, he'd tried to be Mr. Nice Guy to justify being captain. He wanted the guys to like him. Even worse, he'd spent the game terrified of making a mistake — and ended up making a ton of them. You can't play scared, his father had always told him — the best players have the confidence to mess up.

Charlie got dressed and went downstairs.

"Hurry up, Charlie," his mother said. "We have to leave relatively soon — maybe forty-five minutes."

Charlie poured a bowl of cereal. "We could play three games today," Charlie told her. "If we win the first two, we have the quarterfinals tonight."

"Then you'll need an especially good breakfast. Have a little fruit and some toast with that. You need something to stick to your ribs."

Charlie finished his breakfast, grabbed an apple, and went to the garage for his equipment. He was waiting by the car when his mother and sister came out to drive him to the game.

* * *

Charlie didn't talk to anyone while he dressed. The other guys were watching him, but he didn't let on that he noticed. The real Charlie Joyce was going to play this time — not the imposter who worried what others thought. He'd prove his worth on the ice.

Hilton came in, followed by Tremblay.

"Listen up boys," Hilton said. "The less said about last night the better. I can only hope you got it out of your system for the rest of the tournament. Maybe we were overconfident. I don't know. At the very least, you won't have the same excuse for this game. Chesswood is a very good team. They beat us 4–0 last year, and made it to the semifinals. We're going to need a total team effort to win. All three lines need to work hard, and the defence has to clear the front of the net, so Alexi can see the puck.

"We got killed by shots from the point last night. I think at least two goals came from rebounds off point shots. Wingers, you have to be disciplined and stay up high in our own end. That's your responsibility defensively."

Hilton walked over to the blackboard hanging on the wall. He took out a piece of chalk from his pocket and quickly sketched out a series of Xs and Os.

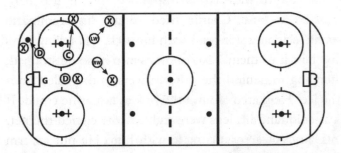

"Let me go over the zone coverage in our end. Assume the other team has the puck deep in the corner. The two wingers stay up high, near the top of the circle, watching the defencemen. One defenceman pressures the puck. The other is in front of the net. The centre cuts off the passing lane, and moves in to pick up the puck if it comes loose. The same applies for the other corner. You just shift over."

Tremblay added, "Don't forget about stick position, boys. You didn't do a great job of it last game. Anticipate where you think the puck will go and get your stick to that spot — and do it with two hands. Alexi, you need to be more aggressive today, especially with the puck in close. Get that paddle down on the ice — hard. Okay?"

Alexi nodded and slapped his pads with his blocker.

Hilton looked around the room. "This is our game to win, boys. This is sudden death. We lose: we're out. So what are we going to do?"

"We're going to take care of business, and then get that gold medal," Scott thundered.

A few of the players responded, but it was half-hearted at best. Charlie tried to get his teammates going, slapping shin pads with his stick, and telling guys to "take it to them." No one was into it, so he stopped, stepping in behind the other players as they filed onto the ice. He skated around the rink as fast as he could. It was cold, and his legs were tight. As he circled the net, Zachary cut across to skate with him. He put an arm around his shoulder.

"This is going to be your game," he said. "Don't be so worried about passing the puck. Use your speed to break them down, and Pudge and me will charge the net and get some traffic in front. We were too fancy last game."

Zachary skated away. Charlie reached out and scooped up a puck lying against the boards. Just then Scott whacked his shin pads with his stick.

"Play your game, bud," he said.

Charlie turned towards the goal for a shot on net. Nick coasted up to him.

"I'm going to be looking for you up the middle in our end. If you can get behind them early, we can get a quick goal."

Charlie shot the puck as the buzzer sounded to end the warm-up. It was clear what his friends thought — and they were right. Mr. Nice Guy was gone. His job was to put the puck in the net, not make pretty passes that went nowhere.

The referee blew his whistle and skated to centre with the puck. Charlie took a final lap around. Jake's line was starting, so Charlie took a seat on the bench between Pudge and Zachary. The three linemates didn't say much to each other. There wasn't much to say. They needed to prove that they deserved to be on the team.

The game started slowly, neither side able to sustain much of an attack. Chesswood certainly knew all about Jake. Charlie watched their centre shadow him around the rink the entire shift, barely paying attention to any other player or the puck. And he was good too. He

could really skate, and seemed to be a hard-nosed player who relished this kind of assignment. Even Jake was
going to have to work hard to get any goals this game,
he thought.

Hilton called Charlie's name. His line was out next.
Liam was carrying the puck across centre, but decided to
dump it in and change. He and Matt peeled off towards
the bench, but Jake continued on to forecheck. He was a
notorious ice hog. Charlie could only hope for a whistle.

His hopes were answered almost immediately.
Chesswood's goalie decided his team needed a change
also, and he covered the puck. Jake looked over at the
bench and reluctantly came off when he saw Charlie
jump over the boards. They skated past each other without saying a word.

"Come on, Charlie. Let's win the draw," Scott
yelled.

Charlie steeled himself, lowered his stick to the circle, and sent the puck spinning back to Scott practically
before it touched the ice. The centre forgot to tie
Charlie up, surprised by losing the draw so cleanly, and
Charlie was able to slip by and charge at the net.

Scott let the puck fly, hard and low to the stick side.
The goalie dropped to his knees and the puck bounced
off his pads right to Charlie. He didn't hesitate a second, sliding hte puck along th eice, just inside the right
post.

The goal came so quickly that the crowd didn't
react at first. Only when his teammates came over to
exchange high-fives and punch gloves did a loud cheer

go up. Charlie felt as if a great weight had been lifted off his shoulders. It wasn't the best goal he'd ever scored, but it sure felt good.

Charlie caught up to Scott.

"Great shot, Mr. Defenceman," he said.

"Nice faceoff, Mr. Joyce."

They started towards the bench, but Hilton waved at them to stay out. Charlie skated over to centre ice for the faceoff. He guessed the centre would be more aggressive on this draw, just after looking so foolish on the goal, and would try to pull the puck back to his defence. Charlie decided to use an old trick. He tied up his opponent's stick before he could pull the puck back, kicked the puck forward between the guy's skates, and spun around to pick it up behind him. The crowd roared its approval, and the Terrence Falls fans cheered Charlie on as he skated in on the two Chesswood defenders.

Neither winger was open, and Charlie was about to dump it in when he remembered his own advice — play with the confidence to make mistakes. Charlie barrelled in, both defencemen holding their ground, determined not to give up the blue line. He faked the dump in, dipped slightly to the left, and slipped the puck in between them, leaping high in the air. The defencemen tried to crush him with their shoulders. All they did was collide into each other. The crowd laughed at the comical sight and the two Chesswood players landed tangled up together on the ice. Charlie was in alone on a breakaway.

He shifted the puck between his forehand and his backhand. That kept the goalie guessing, and he stayed back in his net unsure of what to do. At the hash marks, the puck still on his backhand, Charlie veered sharply across the net, making it look as if he was going to deke to the stick side. The goalie dropped to a butterfly and slid over. Unfortunately for him, that was precisely what Charlie wanted. This was his favourite breakaway move, one he'd practised a thousand times, with his father, in pickup games, street hockey games, and at practice. He turned sideways, hesitated a moment, and then flicked the puck with a backhand over the goalie's shoulder on the glove side.

This time the crowd didn't wait. It let loose a tremendous cheer. Charlie had scored two goals on one shift. His linemates mobbed him as he skated back to the bench.

Much to his surprise, Hilton pointed to centre. He still wanted them out. Chesswood's coach had seen enough, and he sent out a different centre. It didn't slow Charlie and his linemates down, however. Charlie won the draw back to Scott, who slid it across to Nick, who in turn one-timed it to Zachary. The right winger trapped the puck with his skates and banked it off the boards up over centre.

Charlie anticipated the move, and had cut over to take the bank pass. Some Terrence Falls supporters called "get the hat trick," but he wasn't thinking about scoring. Pudge was charging up the middle, and he hit him with a pass a foot before the blue line. Pudge took it in stride and tried to split the defence. They managed to hold him up, but the puck squirted off to the left side. Charlie was on it like a hawk, swerving around to the right to avoid the pile of players. The left defence-man shifted over, straining to keep Charlie outside. Charlie had the puck on his backhand. He took his upper hand off his stick to hold the player off, and cut in on goal.

The goalie wasn't going to let Charlie score again, and he completely overplayed him, straying far over to cut down the angle, even though Charlie had virtually nothing to shoot at, and the puck was on his backhand to boot. Charlie glanced over his shoulder and saw that Zachary had beaten his check to the net. He put his hand back on his stick and flipped the puck across the crease. The goalie was completely out of position, and Zachary one-timed it home for an easy score.

The Terrence Falls fans hooted and hollered for all they were worth. Most of the players were on their feet, high-fiving and slapping their sticks on the boards. The third goal even got a reaction from their usually reserved coach. Hilton clapped a few times — and allowed himself the luxury of a smile.

"Okay, boys, that's enough. Let's get focused. We have lots of hockey to play. Change it up," he said.

The next line went out. Charlie sat down on the bench, thrilled by the goals. Tremblay came over and put a hand on his shoulder.

"That was the Charlie Joyce we've been waiting for," Tremblay said.

"Thanks, Coach," he replied.

"That wasn't a bad shift, boys," Zachary said. "And great play on that goal, Pudge. You were a tank out there. I think you almost killed those defencemen when they tried to hit you."

Pudge blushed. "Charlie gave me a great pass. I couldn't have missed it if I wanted to."

Zachary would have nothing to do with his modesty. "Don't give me that! You keep playing that way and we'll score twenty goals this game. And you set up a beautiful screen for Scott's shot on the first goal."

Pudge was tongue-tied. He managed to mumble, "Thanks," and reached down for a water bottle as an excuse not to say anything more.

"Let's put this game away now," Hilton called out, pacing behind the bench. "One goal, and they're back in it. We have to get the next one, so they know this game's over. Stick to our game plan. Forget the score. It's 0–0, as far as I'm concerned. Get the next goal!"

14

CHELSEA HEATS UP

Their coach need not have worried. Chesswood never recovered from the three quick goals, and the final score was 7–1. Charlie scored another goal early in the third, a slapshot from the slot on a pass from Pudge, giving him three goals and an assist, but he left the ice feeling relieved more than anything. The team had won! The only thing that bothered him was a game misconduct for Jake late in the third. The pesky Chesswood centre continued to shadow Jake even when the score became lopsided. Jake grew so frustrated that he cross-checked his tormentor in the back. That earned him a double minor. He argued the call so loudly that the referee added a misconduct. Jake followed that up by throwing his stick at the penalty box, which was why he got kicked out. He left his stick lying on the ice and stomped off to the dressing room. Chesswood scored its lone goal on the ensuing power play.

The happy mood in the dressing room was a stark contrast to yesterday. Everyone was talking and having a good time, everyone except Jake.

"Can't believe what an idiot that ref was," he complained to Liam. "Guy's a total clown. How many times did I get hooked or held and that jerk was looking right at it?"

"Ref was totally clueless, for sure," Liam sympathized.

"Could you believe that guy, Matt?" Jake said, casting about for support.

Charlie was amazed to see that Matt wasn't paying attention. He turned his back on Jake to listen to Scott describe a run-in with a Chesswood player.

"So he's telling me we got lucky, and it's 6–1 at this point," Scott said.

"He was lucky it wasn't 10–1," Nick said.

"I asked which goals were lucky."

"What did he say?"

"He tells me all six," Scott said, laughing. "So I asked him how many lucky goals did we have to score before they should count. He then tells me to take a hike, and I tell him I'll do that as soon as we score another lucky goal."

"Is that when he cross-checked you and got the penalty?" Matt interjected.

Scott nodded. "That's the best part. I got the pleasure of waving to him after we got the power-play goal. I tried to thank him when he came out of the box, but he wouldn't even look at me. He just kept his head down and skated to the bench."

Hilton held his clipboard up in the air and whistled loudly.

"Can you keep it down a second please? First things first: that was more like it." The players added their own cheers and whistles. "Second thing: we have another game in two hours. Win that and it's into the quarterfinals. Lose and we're out. That makes it easy to figure out what we need to do."

Hilton pointed to two cardboard boxes sitting on the floor.

"We have some sandwiches and drinks, courtesy of Pudge's father, who owns Bruno's Bistro. Help yourself, and drink lots of water. Make sure you get good and hydrated. There are some doughnuts too, supplied by one of the tournament sponsors. Please go easy on those. A dozen donuts is not the best way to get ready for a game.

"Finally, Chelsea is playing next, and it would be a good idea for us to watch. So, unless you have a prior commitment," he said, "why don't you grab something to eat and join Coach Tremblay and me in the stands."

"We'll be the guys with the clipboards," Tremblay quipped.

The game was halfway through the first period by the time everyone got dressed and found a seat. They all sat in one section, surrounding their coaches. As the game progressed, the two hockey men began dissecting the Chelsea team, pointing out their strengths and weaknesses, both as a team and with regard to certain players.

"Take a look at number three, for example," Tremblay said. "Whenever he takes a pass, he looks down at the puck for at least a step or two. That's too long, unless you're absolutely sure no one's near you. So if you're forechecking, get on him real quick. He might not see you coming, and we can get a turnover."

"That number twenty-one looks like a good player, and he's a big guy too." Charlie said. "He's already plowed at least five guys into the boards."

"His name's Burnett," Pudge told him. "He played Peewee Triple-A for the Snow Birds last year. He was the best defencemen in the league, and he came second in scoring to J.C. Savard, which isn't too shabby considering Savard's a centre."

Burnett snapped a pass to his right winger just inside the line. The winger drove into the offensive zone, slowed down at the top of the circle near the boards, and then lofted a soft pass into the high slot back to Burnett, who'd been trailing the play. The defenceman stepped into the pass with a blistering slapshot and the puck streaked into the top left corner. The goaltender barely moved. That made the score 4–0, and the first period was still not over.

"Who's Savard?" Charlie asked.

"You haven't heard of J.C. Savard?" Pudge sounded astonished. "He's the best Bantam player in the district, a regular Wayne Gretzky. He also played for the Snow Birds. Scored something like sixty goals last year, and I think he got even more assists. In my opinion, the only reason we won districts last year," he said, in a lowered tone, "is that he got appendicitis and missed the playoffs. If he's healthy — and the last I heard people only have one appendix — then we're in tough if we play Chelsea."

Charlie watched Savard hop over the boards and join the rush. He called for and received the puck, casually corralling the errant pass out of the air. He circled back towards his own end to gain some room. When the other team's centre tried to poke the puck away, Savard slid it between his legs and cut past, weaving his way through the neutral zone. He gained the blue line and stopped at the top of the right circle, his teammates roaring past. He slid a pass down low to his winger camped out near the side of the net. The goalie and defenceman collapsed on the winger, who feathered a pass back to Savard in the high slot. He wristed it into the top corner, stick side.

It was hard not to admire Savard. Yet, Charlie knew they would have to stop him if Terrence Falls was going to win the gold medal. Although he didn't mean it, he said to Pudge, "He's good, but we can shut him down. We just have to pressure him, knock him around a bit. I'd like to test his toughness. The other team's giving him way too much room. We need to be all over him, as soon as he touches the puck."

Pudge nodded politely, and tried to look confident.

"Coach, I have a question," Charlie said. "Wouldn't you play the trap if you were coaching the other team, and try to keep the score down?"

Hilton thought for a moment. "The trap is a good idea, but I doubt this team could make it work against Chelsea."

He pulled out a sheet of blank paper from a folder and quickly sketched a rink.

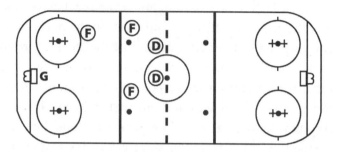

"The concept for the trap is simple. You want to make it difficult to get the puck out along the boards, forcing a team to try risky passes up the middle. It's just a 1–2–2. One player forechecks in deep. The other two forwards line up at the blue line to cut off a breakout pass. The two defencemen back up the forwards, plugging the neutral zone. The tricky part is being able to shift across the ice so that you always have four players in front of the puck. As long as you can force the puck to one side and then stack that side with players, the attacking team will have difficulty breaking through."

He handed the paper to Tremblay. "Why don't you explain how to beat the trap."

"A good rushing defenceman can beat the first forechecker, so he's not pinned to one side," Tremblay said. "He can then use the whole ice, either carrying the puck himself into the neutral zone, or passing to a breaking forward. "Quick passes will also cut the trap to ribbons," Tremblay continued. "You can swing the puck across the ice in your own end, and then move it forward before the other team can set up. The threat of a long pass at another team's blue line also helps stretch the defence and makes it hard for the defencemen to stand near centre. If they drop back to cover, then the neutral zone opens up and it's much easier to break through."

"The trap also requires a fair amount of discipline and timing," Hilton said. "You need to know when to push forward and when to back off. Everyone's movements must be precise, and every player needs to know exactly what to do.

"To state the obvious, we're not watching professionals. They haven't had the time or training to make the trap work. That's why Chelsea's ripping them apart, and why it's already 5–0."

"So they shouldn't play the trap," Charlie conceded. "What should they play?"

"Hopscotch," Scott said.

Hilton laughed, along with the rest of the team. "You might be right, Scott. I don't think they have any real chance of winning. Maybe their only chance would be if Chelsea took the game for granted, but that doesn't seem to be the case."

Charlie watched as Chelsea scored goal after goal. By the third period, Chelsea was trying not to score. Even so, when the game ended, the final tally was 16–0.

A much humbler Terrence Falls team returned to the dressing room compared to the cocky bunch that had left an hour earlier. Charlie was under no illusions about Chelsea. Terrence Falls would have to pick their game up to a whole new level to win.

The door swung open, and Jake, Liam and Thomas came in. It struck Charlie suddenly that they hadn't watched the game with the rest of the team. He noticed that a few of the other players were staring hard at the three boys as well. He wondered if he should say something. He was captain after all, and that kind of thing was not going to foster team spirit — just the opposite, in fact.

The trio sat down in the far corner, joking about how bad Chelsea's opponents had been. Charlie knew it was their way of showing off. Charlie agonized over what to do. Just then the two coaches entered, and Charlie decided not to say anything. He didn't want to start something with the coaches in the room. And, captain or not, he was the last person they'd listen to. It would only make things worse, he reasoned. Charlie opened his bag and pulled out his pants and shin pads. He was relieved. But he also had a nagging feeling that he might have let his team down — again.

15

THE NAME GAME

Charlie enjoyed the cool morning air as he walked along his street to the corner store. He'd been the first one up at home. There was no milk for cereal, so he decided to get some. The night before, his mother had suggested he sleep in, but he couldn't. He was still too worked up about yesterday. Terrence Falls had won all three of its games and made it to the semifinals. In the quarterfinals, with a minute to go and the score tied at two apiece, Charlie intercepted a pass at his own blue line. He had a clear breakaway the length of the ice. As he closed in on the goalie, he spotted Jake out of the corner of his eye, skating hard to catch up. Charlie slowed and drifted to the side. When he got in close, he faked a shot and slipped the puck across the crease. Jake arrived just in time to shovel it into the net. Charlie had also scored the first goal, and set Pudge up for the other, so he'd actually been in on all three goals.

Jake reacted as if he'd scored the goal single-handedly. He jumped up in the air, pumping both arms by his sides. And the heroics continued in the dressing room.

"That team was useless. We just needed some Jake action to seal the deal," he boasted.

Jake was also dissing everybody — Charlie even took a few verbal shots. He could see that some of the guys were not impressed, but he didn't want to ruin the moment by telling Jake off. They'd won, and that was all that counted.

What worried him more than that was how the rift between him and Jake had affected team morale. They played a team called Leaside in the quarterfinals — not a bad squad, but not as good as them. Terrence Falls should have won the game easily. Instead, it had come down to the last minute. Scott, Zachary, Pudge and Nick were barely on speaking terms with Jake, Liam and Thomas. The two groups had made it clear that they wanted nothing to do with each other. He was uncertain about Matt — he'd been fairly quiet lately, and didn't seem to be hanging out with Jake that much. Regardless, team spirit was at an all-time low, with no sign of improvement.

Their semifinal opponent would be Flemington — and they were good. They'd beaten Terrence Falls 4–1 in last year's tournament, and had made it to the finals, where they gave Chelsea a good battle, only losing by one goal. Terrence Falls would never beat Flemington, let alone Chelsea, if things didn't change — and fast! He was thinking of how to fix the problem when he heard his name called out.

"Hey, Charlie. How's it going?"

Charlie looked up. It was one of the guys on the team. For some reason couldn't remember his name.

"It's going okay," Charlie said. "Stoked for the big game?"

"You know it. Except for Chesswood, every game's been so close. Have to admit, there were moments when I didn't think we'd get this far."

"We've gotten lucky — no doubt about that. Better to be lucky than good!"

The boy nodded. "So where're you off to?"

"I'm on a milk run," he said. "Build up the bones before the game, and pack in a few pounds of cereal."

"Sounds like a plan. I'm on a newspaper run. I wanted to check out the hockey scores from last night."

"I don't know who won," Charlie said. "I didn't catch the highlights. I was too tired — just went straight to sleep."

Charlie was desperately trying to remember his name. This was pathetic. He was a forward, probably left wing — but it could be right. He wasn't a defence-man — he was certain of that.

"Do you live near here?" Charlie said.

He looked taken aback. "Actually, I'm about a block down from you, on the same street."

"That's weird. I've never seen you around here."

He shrugged. "I've seen you a few times, going to school and stuff."

The two boys looked at each other.

"Well, I'll see you at the rink," Charlie said.

"Okay. Take it easy."

He crossed the street. Charlie walked into the store, and then it hit him. "Dylan," he said, smacking his forehead. The guy's name was Dylan. Charlie had taken his place in the football game. He was right wing on the third line. How could he have forgotten that? He hoped Dylan hadn't noticed. He must have sounded really dumb when he'd asked where he lived. They were practically next-door neighbours!

He bought the milk and headed home. He didn't enjoy the walk, however. He felt guilty that he'd been playing hockey with Dylan and hadn't said a single word to the guy. He was the new kid, not Dylan — the least he could do was be friendly. How many guys on the team did he really know? he asked himself. There were his friends — Scott, Zachary, Nick and Pudge — and his enemies — Jake and his crew. And while it was kind of awkward to get to know the grade ten guys, he hadn't even made an effort. Some captain!

"I went out for some milk," he announced as he walked into the house.

"Just toss it in the fridge, please."

"No problem, Mom."

Charlie sat at the kitchen table and poured himself a bowl of cereal. He spread out a napkin and grabbed a pen, and then he wrote his name at the top, drawing two large circles underneath. In one circle he listed his friends, and in the other, Jake and his friends. Below those circles he drew a third circle and wrote: *The Rest*. The team's fundamental problem was clear to see. He'd always assumed the team was divided into two. It was actually divided into three.

Suddenly, a plan formed in his mind. He'd been so obsessed about Jake's circle that he'd forgotten there were other guys on the team. He was supposed to be captain for everyone. Maybe it was unrealistic to expect Jake to be his buddy. At the very least he could make his friends and "The Rest" into one circle. Then, at the worst it would be four guys versus thirteen. He decided that from this moment on there'd be no Charlie Joyce clique — not if he could help it.

He folded the napkin and put it in his pocket. He vowed to get started on the plan right away, before their next game, in the dressing room. Time to show the grade tens, and his friends, what kind of captain he could be.

* * *

"Good luck," his grandparents said in unison. They'd come along again to watch the semifinals with his mother and sister.

"Thanks," he said, taking his equipment from the trunk and heading to the arena. He waved back at them and went in. He stopped to watch Chelsea play their semifinal game for a few minutes. It was already 5–0 for Chelsea, with ten minutes left in the second period.

Most of his teammates were getting dressed when Charlie walked into the dressing room. Pudge moved his bag over, and waved for Charlie to sit next to him.

"How are ya?"

"Stoked and ready to go."

Pudge picked up his helmet and rested it on his knee. "Did you catch the score of the Chelsea game?"

Charlie nodded. "As expected, Chelsea's kicking butt. It was 5–0, with about half the second gone."

"They're going to be tough to beat."

"No argument here."

They stopped talking while Charlie dressed. He needed to hustle if he was going to have time to put his plan into action. It didn't take long before he'd pulled his pants on, taped his shin pads, and laced his skates. He took a deep breath and then started to go around the room to each player. His plan was to punch fists with each player, making a point of calling them by their first names, and offer some encouraging words or ask if they were ready to play.

"Go for it, Ethan," he said. "Big game from the D today. Shut 'em down like last game and we'll smoke these boys." He held out his fist and Ethan gave it a punch.

"Let's do it, Adam. Big game from you today. Dylan, I see two goals in your future."

Jake was next. "I didn't get the chance to compliment you on your goal last night," he said. "I didn't think there was any way you could catch up, but you did. I looked over and you were there. It was an awesome hustle."

Charlie held out his fist. This would show everyone that he wanted to end their feud for the good of the team. The room was completely quiet, the atmosphere very tense. Jake stared back momentarily, and then snickered and began taping his shin pads. Charlie lowered his hand slowly, turned, and sat back down. That wasn't good. Pudge raised both eyebrows and didn't say anything. Scott and Nick exchanged surprised looks, but they also kept quiet. Ethan didn't look happy. He shook his head at Jake and reached into his bag for his helmet. Jake's friends were less discreet. Thomas was laughing, and Liam gave Jake the thumbs-up. Charlie noticed, however, that Matt remained silent.

Jake noticed it also, and he said to Matt, "The guy makes one pass a game and thinks he's a superstar."

Matt blinked a few times, cleared his throat, and replied in a low tone, "Give it a rest, Jake. You can be so lame sometimes."

Jake stared long and hard at Matt. "What planet have you moved to, dude? Talk like that to me again, and I'll make sure you'll be eating through a straw for a year."

Matt ignored him, and bent back down to tape his shin pads, which seemed to infuriate Jake even more.

"Big tough guy can't think of anything else to say?"

Matt straightened up, his eyes blazing. "I don't remember asking for your opinion."

"Then make your move, wuss."

Charlie couldn't believe what was going on. After going around the room he'd planned on making a speech about how the team had to pull together if it wanted to win. Things couldn't have gone worse. He'd underestimated just how much Jake hated him, and he also hadn't considered how Jake's friends would react.

Charlie knew that neither player was likely to back down. Jake was a tough customer. But Matt couldn't be intimidated, either. He wasn't as big as Jake, but his powerful build made him an imposing figure when provoked.

Charlie tried to get them to calm down. "Guys, let's be cool," he said. "This is insane. We're only one game away from the final. This isn't the time."

Jake looked over at him. "Actually, it's time that I busted you up, once and for all. I'm tired of seeing your face, and I'm tired of putting up with your garbage."

Jake charged him. Charlie was too shocked to move. Before Jake could throw a punch, however, Matt body-checked him from the side, knocking him into the wall. Jake fell to the floor, but was back on his feet in a second.

"You're as good as dead, Danko," he yelled.

Before he could charge again, Charlie got up and stood next to Matt.

"So I'll take both of you losers on," Jake snarled.

Then Pudge got up and stood next to them, followed by Scott, Nick and Zachary. Ethan came over, as did the rest of the grade tens.

"You were saying, Wilkenson?" Ethan said quietly.

That stopped Jake in his tracks. "You guys are real brave when it's ten against one," he said.

"I think that's more your style, Jake," Matt said.

"I think I'd rather jump out of an airplane without a parachute than play with you jerks," he said.

"Let me book your flight," Scott said.

A few titters of laughter were followed by a few more, until most of the guys were roaring. Charlie watched Jake closely. He half expected him to take them all on. He didn't. Instead, with a cocky grin on his face, he picked up his bag and said, "Liam, Thomas, I'm tired of carrying this loser of a team. Let's go. It stinks in here, anyway."

Jake left, followed by his two friends.

"If you ask me, it smells a lot better now," Scott quipped.

That set the guys off again, but they quieted down when the coaches walked in and reality sunk in.

"I just saw Jake, Liam and Thomas leaving with their equipment," Hilton said. "Would someone like to tell me what's going on?"

Charlie felt all eyes on him. He cleared his throat to stall for time. "I don't think they want to play for the team," he said finally.

Hilton took a deep breath, shaking his head.

He looked around the room.

"Here's what we'll do. We've got five defencemen, so one guy will sit every second shift. Up front, we have two lines and a sub. Dylan, you go through the lines on the wing. Matt and Charlie will be the centres. I just have to speak to the convener about the lineup changes."

Hilton and Tremblay left. Charlie didn't know what to say to the team, but he had to say something. He had initiated the fight to some extent by going up to Jake in the first place. But he still thought he'd done the right thing. Jake, Liam and Thomas made the decision to quit. That wasn't his doing. Unfortunately, the fight seemed to drain the energy out of the team. Everyone was quiet, looking down at the floor or straight ahead at the walls. What could he do with this lifeless bunch?

While Charlie considered his options, the Chelsea players filed past the dressing room. Some of the players began chanting, "Six in a row!" Obviously, they'd won. The chant grew louder until all the Chelsea players and the coaches were joining in.

The Terrence Falls players sat glumly, listening to their rivals. Charlie cupped his hands around his mouth, and bellowed at the top of his lungs, "Wait till you play a real team. And bring your silver shoes to match the silver medal you'll get. Terrence Falls gets the gold!"

That got a reaction.

"Has Terrence Falls ever won anything?" one Chelsea player hooted.

"I don't see you even getting to the finals," said another.

"We'll try to keep the score under 10–0 for ya."

That was too much for an avid trash-talker like Scott. "You're living in the past, dudes. You'd better hope we go easy on you."

"Come and see my trophy case, big man," a Chelsea player responded.

"You really know how to party," Scott mocked.

His teammates joined in, and soon both teams were trading insults back and forth. The Chelsea coach eventually hustled his team into their dressing room, and the hallway was quiet. Not the Terrence Falls dressing room, though — all the players were on their feet, fired up for the game.

Zachary jumped up on the bench. "Play with reckless abandon, boys," the normally laid-back winger said. "If you don't break a bone, you're not trying!"

"Safe with the puck," Craig chimed.

"Leave it all on the ice today," Ethan said.

"And play smart. No stupid penalties."

"Let's go out and hammer these guys."

"They can't keep up if we play our game."

"Sudden death, guys. No sense worrying about tomorrow."

Charlie held up his hand and the room quieted. "I don't think anyone gives us a chance without Jake, Liam and Thomas. But, to tell you the truth, I didn't think we had a chance of winning with them. I think we just got a whole lot better. We go hard right from the start. We win this game one shift at a time. And it starts with the drop of the puck."

He looked at Alexi. "How about you lead us onto the ice, so we can win this thing already."

The goaltender flipped his mask down and marched down the hall. Charlie held the door open and hit each player's shoulder pads as they passed.

"Let's go, Scott. Your game, Ethan. Come on, Nick. Take it to them, Pudge. Work hard, Dylan . . ."

Charlie was last to leave. He cast a glance at the empty dressing room. Could they really win without three of their best players? Frankly, he wasn't sure.

16

SHORT BENCH

Terrence Falls came out strong, and dominated most of the game, firing shot after shot at the Flemington goalie. He'd played an outstanding game, however, and the score remained tied at 0–0 deep in the third period — but he'd also been lucky. Nick had banged one off the post early in the first period, and Zachary had missed on an open net to start the third.

With less than three minutes to play, a Flemington defenceman had the puck at his blue line. His left winger cut across the neutral zone.

"Simon, quick pass," he said.

The winger took the pass, but Charlie was right on him, and he was forced to circle to his end, where he dropped the puck back to his defenceman. He decided to try it himself this time, and headed down the left side. Pudge saw that and cut him off, which left him with little choice but to fire it in.

Charlie took advantage to call for a change, which is why he didn't see the puck career off Pudge's skate.

Pudge dropped to the ice, clutching his foot, and the whistle blew.

Charlie assumed the puck had gone out of play and didn't turn around.

"Pudge got hurt," Matt said, pointing to the ice.

Charlie's heart sank. Pudge had played such a solid game to that point. He followed the trainer over to his friend.

"You gonna make it?" Charlie asked.

"Zachary said if you don't break a bone, you're not trying."

"Please don't tell me your foot's broken."

"Let's find out."

"Wait a minute," the trainer said. He probed gently. "Okay, try putting some weight on it."

Charlie helped him up. Pudge slowly lowered his skate to the ice. He winced, leaning on Charlie for support. "Not too bad," he said. "I've had worse."

Pudge glided to the bench, with the trainer's help, but he kept most of his weight on his other foot. Charlie started slapping the ice with his stick and was soon joined by the other players. Matt hopped the boards and skated to Charlie.

"We didn't need that," Matt said.

"Tell me about it," Charlie replied.

"Not much time left. We need to take it up a notch and put this game away."

"It's time for you to be the hero."

Matt grinned. "Now that you mention it, I do feel heroic all of a sudden."

Charlie rapped his shin pads and joined Pudge on the bench.

"Do you think you can play?" Charlie asked.

He looked uncertain. "The pain's gone away a bit. I think I'll give it a try and see what happens."

Charlie looked up. A Flemington defenceman had the puck at centre, and he fired it down the ice to get a change. He turned back to Pudge. "We need you out there. It would be huge if you could tough it out."

A roar from the crowd interrupted, and he heard the whistle blow.

"What happened?" he asked Zachary.

"I think this team's cursed. Alexi caught the puck, and went to sweep it behind the net to Scott. The problem is, he swept it right into our net," Zachary said.

"They scored?"

"It appears so."

The Flemington players had their sticks over their heads, most of them laughing, pounding the scorer's back.

Hilton pulled lightly on Charlie's shoulder pads.

"How about you go out there and tie this game up?" he said.

Charlie jumped over the boards and headed straight to Alexi. He had dropped to his knees, head down. He looked up at Charlie, unable to say a word.

"We wouldn't be here without you," Charlie said, giving his pads a whack. "And what's done is done. Let's make a deal, you and me. I'll get that one back, if you promise not to let another goal in for the rest of the game."

Charlie knew Alexi was ultra-competitive. He even hated giving up a goal in practice, so that challenge was music to his ears. He loved to be counted on, to come through in the clutch. Some players shrink from that responsibility. Not Alexi, and Charlie was counting on it.

Alexi hit his own pads with his stick, and jumped to his feet. He crouched down to show he was ready, "You get that goal," he said. "Scoring is over for them."

The next two minutes were complete and utter mayhem. The puck barely left Flemington's end. The Terrence Falls players played like madmen, desperately trying to set up a good scoring chance. Flemington held on bravely, launching their bodies in front of shots and diving after every loose puck. With thirty seconds left, Terrence Falls was still behind by one, and the faceoff was deep in Flemington's end to the goalie's left. Hilton pulled Alexi, allowing Matt to join the attack.

Charlie circled around to stall for time, struggling to catch his breath. His spirits got a big boost when Pudge came out to take over left wing. Scott and Nick were on the point, with Zachary on the wing against the boards. He felt good about the six guys out there — each had proved himself to be a hockey warrior in this game. It occurred to him that they were all grade nines. He looked over at the bench. His older teammates were on their feet banging the boards and calling out encouragement. They were counting on them to tie it up, and proving to be unselfish by not complaining about ice time. Regardless of whether they scored, Charlie felt that for the first time they were a real team — all pulling together to try to win.

The referee blew his whistle and held the puck aloft. Charlie drifted to the faceoff and choked up on the stick to make it look as if he wanted to draw the puck back to the point. Before the puck was dropped, though, he glanced sharply at Zachary and hit the ice twice with his stick.

That signal meant Charlie would tie the centre up, rather than try to win the draw. Zachary would come over and dig the puck out for a quick shot on goal. Zachary anticipated the drop of the puck, swept across, and in one motion fired a bullet to the short side. The goalie got a piece of it with his left pad, deflecting it to the corner.

The Flemington defenceman got to the puck first, but Charlie, who had spun loose from the centre, was right on him. The defenceman panicked and shot the puck up the boards before his winger was ready, and the puck continued on to Nick, who trapped it inside the line. Nick blasted it back down along the boards, all the way around the net to the far corner, where Pudge was waiting.

Pudge got control of the puck, but he didn't have a chance to pass it before Flemington's right defenceman was on him. The two players battled for possession, but neither was able to knock the puck free. Matt joined them, along with Flemington's right winger. Charlie looked up at the clock in frustration. Only twenty seconds remained. He skated behind the net to see if he could help. Pudge saw him, and, with a Herculean effort, bulled his way forward, dislodging the puck momentarily, which let Matt kick it free to Charlie.

Charlie snatched the puck and skated backwards with it behind the net, looking around to assess the situation. Zachary was banging with the left defenceman in front trying to establish position. The defenceman was a big, strong kid and gave no quarter. Charlie doubted Zachary would ever get his stick down for a pass. He would have to come up with something else, and fast.

Nick waved his stick in the air at the point, and Charlie was on the verge of passing it to him, when the Flemington centre moved over to block the passing lane. Scott drifted into the slot area, but he was quickly covered by the left winger. With ten seconds left, the crowd began to count down. When they reached seven, Charlie decided his only option was the wraparound. Unfortunately, Flemington's solid positional play made that impossible. The right defenceman had raced over to cover the left post, and the right winger was covering the right post.

He heard the count reach five, and then decided to try something he'd seen an NHL player do once. Charlie came out the left side, as if he was going to go for the wraparound. The defenceman flopped to the ice to block his path, and then extended his arms and legs so Charlie couldn't pass it in front anywhere. Charlie had no intention of passing, however. He flicked the puck high in the air, over the prone defenceman, to the very spot where he'd been covering, three feet from the top of the crease. He then jumped over the defenceman and twisted around in the air, so that he was facing the net. Charlie and the puck landed at the same time. The goalie had dropped to his knees to prevent Charlie from stuffing it in on the short side. That left the top of the net open. He swung his stick, and the puck sailed over the goalie's shoulder, into the top corner. Charlie had passed the puck to himself and, as if by miracle, had tied the game with two seconds left.

The entire team poured off the bench and piled onto him. Everyone was banging on each other's helmets and exchanging high-fives. Charlie was just trying to breathe, crushed under a pile of players. But he loved it all the same, and, like his delirious teammates, could hardly believe he had scored.

The referees broke up their celebrations to remind them that the game was tied. There were still two seconds on the clock, and then a five-minute overtime. If that didn't settle it, there would be a shootout.

The late goal deflated the Flemington squad. For most of the overtime it looked like they were just trying to get it over with. They dumped the puck into Terrence Falls' end almost as soon as they crossed centre, dropping back to play defence. That made it difficult for Terrence Falls to get anything going. The play was choppy as a result, with lots of turnovers and constant whistles. The buzzer sounded, ending the overtime, without either team coming close to scoring.

A referee came over to Hilton to explain the rules.

"You need to pick three shooters. Have them wait behind the red line on the ice. Non-shooters stay on the bench. The shooters will go in on a breakaway from centre, alternating between each team. Whichever team gets the most goals wins. If it's still tied after three shooters, then we keep going until one team scores and the other doesn't. Understood?"

Hilton nodded and the referee skated away. He leaned over and said something to Tremblay, who whispered something back. After that brief exchange, Hilton announced who the shooters would be.

"Okay, fellas. This is the first group of shooters, and I want you to go in this order: Charlie, Zachary, Matt."

Those three players stayed on the ice while everyone else filed onto the bench.

"Don't try to make the perfect move," Hilton told the shooters. "Just don't get cheated. That's the important thing. Watch the goalie and, by the top of the circle, you should know if you're going to shoot or deke. If you shoot, shoot hard. If you deke, make it a strong move. Now let's get this thing over with."

They nodded in unison and shuffled to their spot behind the red line.

The referee came over to them. "You guys are the visitors for this game, so you go first."

Charlie skated slowly to centre. He took a deep breath. He had decided what to do the second the coach called his name. His father had taught him long ago that one of the hardest shots for a goalie to stop on a breakaway is along the ice on the stick side. It's also difficult for the shooter, because if the puck lifts even an inch or two the goalie can make an easy pad save. Done right, however, it's nearly impossible to stop.

Flemington's goalie was more aggressive than he'd been all game, and he came out to challenge Charlie. Charlie considered changing his mind, but his coach's advice came back to him. Don't get cheated. At the hash marks, Charlie drew his stick back and snapped a hard shot along the ice to the stick side. The goalie didn't even move, as the puck streaked into the corner.

Charlie pumped his arm in the air. The other shooters skated over, rewarding him with several slaps to the helmet. Now it was Flemington's turn. Their first shooter wasted no time. He carried the puck in at top speed, faked to his forehand, and lofted a backhand towards the top corner. Alexi was not fooled. He had come out to cut down the angle, and slid across in a butterfly to stop the puck with his right shoulder.

The Terrence Falls fans roared their approval, while the Flemington side groaned. Zachary was up next. He moved in, deked to his right, and slid the puck between the goalie's legs to pot the second goal. Flemington's second shooter slapped the ice with his stick to fire himself up. He slowed as he crossed the blue line, drifting in and firing a hard shot at the five-hole between Alexi's legs. Alexi flopped to the ice, and the puck hit him in the stomach.

He'd been as good as his word. Flemington hadn't scored again.

Charlie was too stoked to react. Not so his teammates who pounded him on the helmet and chanted, "Ter-rence Falls! Ter-rence Falls! Ter-rence Falls!" Despite everything that had happened, they had earned the right to face Chelsea in the finals.

17

SHADOW

A large, round-faced man wearing a crisp, short white coat and a happy grin on his face greeted Charlie as he filed off the bus. Charlie guessed he was Bruno Moretti, the owner and main attraction of Bruno's Bistro, one of Terrence Falls' most popular restaurants, and also Pudge's father. Bruno had generously invited the entire team for lunch after the game, an offer gratefully accepted by both coaches who thought it would be good for the players to stay together.

"I've made spaghetti with lots of tomato sauce," Pudge's father said, "but not too heavy. No meat. And I also made nice salad. And for dessert, fruit."

"That's terrific," Hilton said, as they walked together into the bistro.

Bruno nodded graciously. "Ricardo, Tony, they're here. Let's bring out the food."

A long table had been set up for them in the middle of the mainly empty restaurant. The players took their seats, talking about the Flemington game and the approaching showdown against Chelsea. Pudge's foot was of great concern to everyone. It was beginning to swell up. He was limping noticeably, and had trouble putting any weight on it.

When Bruno saw Pudge, he clutched his hair and moaned and made a terrible fuss. "Oh my goodness, look at that foot. It's the size of a watermelon. This is terrible, terrible. And just before the final. I saw you get hit, but never thought it would be this bad. Let me get some ice. That's what we need. Lots and lots of ice. Tony, get me a bucket of ice and a towel."

"Dad, it's not that serious. Besides, I already put some ice on it after the game."

"It's probably a good idea," Hilton said. "Let's keep icing it, and see how it goes."

"We'll get you fixed up for the final," Bruno said. "The Morettis are tough."

Tony brought the bucket. Pudge was embarrassed by his father's attention, but he dutifully let him wrap the ice around his foot. While that was going on, Scott asked the coaches how they were planning to shut down Chelsea's high-powered offence.

"We have some ideas about that," Hilton said. "Let's have lunch and relax first." He pointed at the kitchen as Ricardo and Tony came out carrying two large trays with steaming hot plates of spaghetti.

"Help yourselves to the parmigiano," Bruno told them. "And we'll bring out a few pitchers of pop and some water."

He hit his forehead with his hand. "What was I

thinking? Two trays are not enough for hungry hockey players. Ricardo, get two more, and lots of sauce. Coach, we got lots of fruit, too. I'll get that now. Good for energy. They'll need it against Chelsea. I saw them play before you. Good team. Very fast — very skilled. But we'll win. We play more together."

"I think you're right, Bruno. And some fruit would be great. You're being too good to us. Thanks again."

"Nothing's too good for the gold-medal team," he said.

Hilton just smiled.

"Now what's taking so long with that pasta? Ricardo, what you doing in there?" Bruno yelled. He went off to the kitchen to see for himself.

There was a lull in the conversation, as the players settled down to eat their lunch. Charlie was sitting across from Hilton, and he decided to take advantage of the quiet to ask a question — one he'd been dying to ask since he heard Liam say that Hilton once had a try-out with the Boston Bruins.

"Excuse me, Coach," Charlie began. "Can I ask you a question?"

Hilton held up a hand. "We'll get to our strategy against Chelsea in due course — don't worry. Let's enjoy this wonderful food, and then we'll get down to business.

"It's not about the game," Charlie said hesitantly.

"Then ask away," he said, taking a sip of water.

"I was wondering, and I think a bunch of us were wondering, what happened to your hockey career after

Terrence Falls? I know you played junior, and did really well, but I don't know much after that."

Hilton pursed his lips, took another sip of water, and looked straight at him. Charlie instantly regretted asking the question. The coach clearly didn't want to talk about it.

But then, suddenly, Hilton's features softened, and he nodded slightly. "What, specifically, did you want to know?"

Charlie's question had caught everyone's attention, and all the players were waiting for their coach to answer. Speculating on his hockey past was a favourite pastime. His scoring records with the Watford Park Rangers had stood for over twenty years, until Karl Schneider broke them only the year before. Little was known about Hilton's playing days apart from that. He was an intensely private man and he rarely spoke about himself.

"I heard that you were drafted by an NHL team."

"I was," he said. "I'm afraid it's not much of a story. I was drafted by the Boston Bruins."

"What round?" Charlie interrupted.

Hilton smiled. "The first round."

Charlie was surprised to hear that. Liam had said Hilton hadn't done anything. The first round was incredible — how many players could say that?

"So the Bruins drafted me, which was pretty cool because they were a very good team back then. It was after the glory days of Bobby Orr and Phil Esposito, but still they could play. I was only eighteen, and was still eligible for another year of junior, but the team invited me to training camp."

"What was that like?" Charlie asked.

"It was quite the experience. The Bruins used to play in the Boston Gardens, a classic old arena. It had an amazing atmosphere — it was a thrill just skating in that building. And like I said, the Bruins were a solid team. They had guys like Rick Middleton, Raymond Bourque, Keith Crowder, Charlie Simmer, Kenny Linseman, Cam Neely." He laughed. "You may not have heard of them, since none of you were born back then, but they were stars at the time."

"I've heard of Bourque," Scott said.

"Me too," Charlie chimed.

"He played a long time," Hilton acknowledged. "Anyway, given the talent on the ice, and the fact that I was so young, I never expected to make the team. But I lasted the entire training camp, and played in several exhibition games. We had a few injuries going into the regular season, and management decided to keep me up until the regulars returned."

"So you got to play in the NHL."

"I did. Not for too long, unfortunately. In my third game, I got hurt, and was never able to play again."

He paused and took another sip of water. "Sorry that it's such a dull story," he joked, "but that's what happened. Unlike some guys, I always took school seriously, and only had one year to get my high school diploma. I came back to Terrence Falls, finished high school, and then went on to university, where I studied to be a teacher — and the rest, as they say, is history."

"How'd you get hurt?" Charlie asked.

"We were in Chicago. It was in the first period, early in the game. There was a scramble in front of the net. I was in the slot, waiting for the puck to come free. Someone shot the puck, I think it was Middleton, and it bounced over to me. I had to stretch to get it, putting all my weight on my left leg. I was way off balance, but still got the shot off. The second I let it go, however, I was submarined by a defenceman. He hit that left leg, tearing the ACL completely, and even breaking the kneecap. I had surgery the next day, but they couldn't fix all the damage. Despite all the rehab — and I really went at it — I never got all my strength or flexibility back. The knee just couldn't take the punishment of professional hockey."

Charlie interrupted the silence that followed Hilton's story. "Did you score on that last shot?" he asked.

"Actually, I did," Hilton replied, with a hint of pride.

Charlie looked at him with a new sense of admiration. It was one thing to be an excellent English teacher and a superb coach. Getting drafted in the first round was also impressive. Scoring in an NHL game was another matter entirely.

"I read once that in the history of hockey only six thousand men have ever played in an NHL game. At least you're one of those guys," Charlie said.

"I've never heard that," Hilton said. "I like the sound of it, though."

Bruno came storming out of the kitchen holding yet another large tray of pasta. "Who needs more? Come on. I know some of you are still hungry. Put up your hand if you want a little extra."

A few players held up empty plates and Bruno scurried to fill them.

"Eat up, boys. I've got lots and lots. Don't be shy with Bruno. You need your energy."

Bruno buzzed around the table, fussing over the players, encouraging them to eat, filling their glasses, and taking away the dirty dishes. He made a special effort to meet Charlie, asking about his mother's café, and promising to try it out as soon as it opened. Charlie liked him. He seemed genuine and sincere, just like his son.

"Say, does anyone know how the other Terrence Falls teams did?" Pudge asked.

"I think our senior boys' team got through to the finals," Nick offered. "They play tonight after our game."

"What about the girls' teams?" Charlie asked.

Nick winked. "Any team in particular you wanna know about?"

"How about both of them?"

"Senior team lost in the quarterfinals. The junior team is playing before us for the gold medal."

"Terrence Falls could win three golds," Charlie said. "It's not four, but enough to make Karl Schneider happy, I'm sure."

"Guess what else?" Nick said. "Schneider is the

leading scorer in the senior tournament. And our friend here, Mr. Charlie Joyce, is in third place for the junior division, behind J.C. Savard and Burnett. We just need to pump the rubber past that chump of a Chelsea goalie and we'll have three gold medals and two leading scorers."

"Let's not count our chickens before they hatch," Hilton interrupted. "Terrence Falls has some serious teams to beat before claiming all that gold."

He rapped a spoon on the table. "Everyone listen up, please. It looks like you pigs have finally finished stuffing yourselves. And for those of you still eating, that's enough. You're playing in three hours, so give your stomachs a chance to digest. Coach Tremblay and I would appreciate it greatly if you would make your way over to the private dining room in the back. We would like to go over a few things before the game, and Bruno needs to clear this table."

Charlie got up with the others, but Hilton motioned for him to stay behind.

"I just need a quick word with Charlie," he said, as the players left.

"I'm sorry about asking you about your hockey career. I was just wondering — that's all."

Hilton waved it off. "You don't have to apologize. To be honest, I hadn't thought about it in a long time — it brought back some great memories. But that's not why I wanted to talk to you. I need you to do something for me, and it relates to what Nick was saying about the scoring lead," Hilton said. "First off, you're ten points behind Savard, so catching him will be some-what difficult. In any event, the team needs you to do something, which will make it impossible for you to catch either Savard or Burnett."

Charlie couldn't imagine what it was.

"I believe the key to beating Chelsea is to keep those two from scoring. We shut those two down, and we have a good shot. I think we can handle Burnett with the right forechecking strategy, which is what Coach Tremblay is going over right now. We'll send two men on him whenever he touches the puck and force him to pass. In our end, the winger on his side will stay up high and keep the puck off his stick."

He placed his clipboard on the table, looking at Charlie intently.

"That doesn't really concern you, though." He held up his hand in response to Charlie's quizzical look. "Savard is much tougher to shut down," he continued. "He's too fast to control by forechecking. He roams all over, is very unpredictable and, to top it off, very smart with and without the puck. That's why I don't think the team approach will work. The trap, the left-wing lock, it doesn't matter. We don't do those things well enough anyway. And without Jake and Liam, we also don't have two powerful forward lines to put out against him."

He stopped and placed his hand on the back of Charlie's chair. "The only way we can stop Savard is to put someone on him, a shadow, a player who will follow him all over the ice, never let him free for a moment, not even in Chelsea's end. This player has to forget about scoring, about doing anything other than keeping the puck off Savard's stick. And that player is you, Charlie," he stated bluntly. "You're the only one with the skills to match him. But it also means you won't be scoring many goals."

"I don't care about that, Coach," he said. "I'd be happy to do it, if you think that's the best way to win."

"I had a feeling you'd say that." Hilton paused for a moment. "Before we join the others, I wanted to tell you that I think you've done a terrific job as captain. I really mean that. I know it hasn't been easy. In fact, it's been the opposite of easy. So I'm very proud of how you've handled yourself. You've earned the title."

"Thanks, Coach," Charlie said, uncomfortable with the praise.

"One more thing," Hilton said, rising from the table. "Since Jake and Thomas quit the team, I don't feel an obligation to keep this from you. Jake got only three first place votes for captain. Thomas didn't get any. I thought you'd like to know how solidly the guys are behind you."

He left Charlie at the table and hurried to the back of the restaurant to join the strategy session. Charlie got up slowly, digesting what his coach had told him about the voting. Charlie had voted for Ethan. Presumably Liam and Thomas had voted for Jake. That accounted for three of the four votes. He'd always assumed Matt voted for Jake, which would make that three. But then there was Jake's vote to consider. Jake didn't vote for Thomas, because he hadn't gotten any votes, and he certainly didn't vote for Charlie Joyce! He must have voted for himself, which meant that Matt didn't vote for Jake. He must have voted for Charlie, along with every player still on the team.

He walked over to join his teammates. Matt was sitting at the back, off to the side. Charlie sat down quietly next to him. Tremblay was explaining the forechecking strategy. Charlie looked over at Matt. Obviously the rift between Jake and him was deeper, and had existed a lot longer, than he'd previously suspected.

Matt caught his eye. He leaned over, and asked, "What did the coach want?"

Charlie lowered his voice. "I'm going to shadow Savard for the whole game."

"Good idea. You'll shut him down."

"I'm going to need a lot of help. He's a serious hockey player."

Matt didn't reply, and Charlie turned his attention to Tremblay. He felt a tug on his shirt.

"Hey, I want to apologize for some of the stuff I did, with Jake and those guys," Matt said. "We were just being jerks, and I feel bad about it. They've been jerks for a while, if you ask me, but I didn't have the guts to walk away. We were friends since kindergarten, and . . ." Matt didn't finish. He looked down at the floor and shook his head.

Charlie considered his words carefully before answering. "Forget about it. I'm glad you're on the team — and I appreciate what you did in the dressing room."

Matt was about to reply when Hilton interrupted. "Guys, would you listen up, please? I don't want to have to repeat myself."

Every so often someone would raise his hand to ask a question, but for the most part the players were content to listen. The nerves were beginning to kick in. The chalk talk made the game seem imminent — and it was a game few people gave them a chance of winning. Chelsea had destroyed every team it played, while Terrence Falls had struggled just to make the final.

Matt leaned over to Charlie and whispered, "This game's going to come down to which team wants it more."

Charlie looked at his teammates. Scott, the jokester, was all business. Nick was jotting down some notes. Zachary, who rarely showed any emotion, was bolt upright in his chair, focused intently on what was being said. The dependable Pudge was gingerly testing his foot, grimacing a little, but still paying close attention.

He whispered back to Matt, "If it comes down to that, we'll win."

18

DEADLOCK

"Ter-rence Falls, Ter-rence Falls!"

"Chel-sea, Chel-sea, Chel-sea!"

Supporters for both teams waved signs and chanted their school names while they waited for the game to start. On the ice, the players were finishing their warm-up. Shots were being fired in on the goalies. A few players sat down on the ice to stretch. Charlie stood near the bench, next to Pudge and Scott. They were all breathing heavily, having just sprinted around the rink several times.

Charlie felt those familiar butterflies in his stomach. He was glad they were there, because he knew it meant he was ready. He always felt uneasy before a big game. Scott handled the stress as only he could — talking a mile a minute.

"We've got to come out hard. They think they've already won the game. Look at them prancing around the ice like little princes."

Scott tapped Pudge on the shin pads.

"Is the foot okay?"

"Hurts a little, but no worries."

"Good. You need to introduce some of them Chelsea babies to the bodycheck. If we get physical early, without taking stupid penalties, it'll set the tone. If they dictate the play to us, we're dead. Got to play our game, right Charlie?"

Charlie half-laughed, amused by Scott's compulsion to chatter away. Only the referee's whistle silenced him. The Terrence Falls players crowded around Alexi, whacking his pads and rubbing his head for good luck. Chelsea's coach decided not to start J.C. Savard, perhaps hoping Terrence Falls would start its best players and Savard could go out against a lesser line. Hilton didn't fall for that. He told Charlie to come to the bench and wait for Savard.

Charlie was relieved not to start. It gave him a chance to calm down. He took a sip of water and yelled a few words of encouragement to Matt, who was starting at centre. The referee waved to the goalies, and both waved back that they were ready. He then held the puck over his head, brought it down slowly, and dropped it to start the game.

The crowd roared its approval. They were ready for some action, and Chelsea gave it to them. They controlled the puck off the faceoff and quickly dumped it into Terrence Falls' end. Scott retrieved it in the corner. A forechecker steamed in on him. He took a look up ice and then passed the puck behind the net, believing Nick would be there. Unfortunately, Nick had decided to stay in front of the net and cover the centre. Craig was late getting to the boards and the puck got by him completely.

The puck caromed around the boards and out to the blue line to Burnett. He corralled the puck and pushed forward at the net. Craig charged at him — exactly what Hilton told them not to do. Burnett was a magnificent stickhandler, and he slipped the puck between Craig's legs, carving sharply around him. That left only Nick between him and the goal. Burnett raised his stick for a slapshot. Nick flung himself on the ice to block it. Burnett had faked the shot, however. He stepped around Nick, and went in alone on Alexi. He came out to challenge the shooter, which left Chelsea's centre, whom Nick had been covering, alone in front. Once Alexi had committed to the shot, Burnett slid the puck across. Scott came roaring over from the corner, but he was too late. Chelsea's centre redirected the pass into the gaping net. Twenty seconds into the game, and Chelsea had already drawn first blood.

The Chelsea fans clapped and chanted the school name. It looked like the rout was on, and a few of the more boisterous ones taunted the Terrence Falls fans.

"At this rate, the score will be a hundred to nothing by the end of the first," one of them boasted.

"We should have played a grade six team. This just isn't fair."

"Hey, I think Hilton is crying. Just wait until we score our tenth goal — in this period!"

Hilton was far from crying. He was busy rallying his

troops after the disastrous start.

"No big deal, guys. It was a bad goal. The game starts now. Who's going to get that one back?"

"We'll take care of it," Charlie said, nodding to his linemates. He'd seen J.C. Savard step onto the ice, and knew his line was up.

He headed to centre. The butterflies were still there. Usually they were gone once the game started, but not this time. He was as nervous as ever. Savard had choked up on his stick with a reverse grip, and was hunched over the faceoff spot. Charlie guessed that meant he would try to draw the puck back to his defenceman. He decided to tie him up and let Zachary swing by and pick it up. He gave Zachary the signal and moved in.

The puck was dropped, but instead of pulling it back, Savard pushed the puck between Charlie's legs. The move took him completely by surprise. Savard slipped around him and broke in on the defence. He faked a move outside, and then sliced in between the defenceman with lightning speed. Both defencemen tried vainly to head him off, but his move had left them flat-footed, and he burst past them and roared in alone on a breakaway.

Charlie hustled gamely after him, furious that he'd fallen for one of his own favourite moves. Alexi drifted far out of his net, almost recklessly. Savard saw that, and deked to his backhand. Alexi anticipated the move and flung his left pad tight against the post in a butterfly. Savard tried to backhand it over Alexi's shoulder, but Alexi was there, thrusting his big blocker out and knocking the puck harmlessly to the corner.

Savard swerved to retrieve the puck, with Charlie close behind. Savard scooped the puck onto his backhand, looking over his shoulder for a teammate. Charlie veered the same way, cutting off the passing lane to the front of the net. He played the body completely — no more trying to outguess this superstar. Savard tried to double back behind the net and Charlie rode him into the boards, holding him there until Nick retrieved the puck and rattled it off the boards and out of their end.

Savard skated away, shaking his head and slapping his stick on the ice, angry at missing the breakaway. Charlie followed behind closely, shaking his head also, disgusted with himself for messing up on his first shift. From now on, he'd stick to the basics — Savard was too good and, as he'd just shown, one mistake could prove costly.

To the surprise of the Chelsea fans, and most likely the Terrence Falls fans as well, the rest of the period passed by without another goal. The early goal did not dishearten the Terrence Falls squad. If anything, it hardened their resolve to play tough and not give an inch. Some monumental battles for the puck took place in all four corners, and more often than not, a Terrence Falls player came away with it.

Charlie worked especially hard to kept Savard from touching the puck. Savard had been shadowed his entire life. That was nothing new for him, but it looked like he wasn't used to being shadowed by someone as good as Charlie. The only drawback for Terrence Falls was that

Charlie couldn't contribute on offense. They barely mounted an attack. The most action the Chelsea goalie saw was passing the puck to the referee after an icing. Chelsea continued to have some good chances, but the acrobatic Alexi kept them off the score sheet.

Chelsea got lucky at the start of the second period. Pudge was in Chelsea's end pressuring a defenceman who was trying to skate the puck out of the zone. Pudge swung his stick at the puck, but inadvertently clipped the defender's skates, sending him tumbling to the ice. He didn't mean to do it, but the referee had no choice — his arm went up to signal a penalty.

"Don't sweat it," Charlie said to Pudge, as he went to the penalty box. "Just another bad break. We'll kill this off."

Charlie and Zachary stayed on, and Scott and Nick came out on defence. Charlie had been holding his own against Savard in the faceoff department, after he'd been beaten so badly on the first shift. He went in hard, hoping to get the puck back to Scott so he could fire it deep into Chelsea's end. Savard had his own idea, however, and once more showed Charlie just how clever he could be. Savard didn't try to win the draw, but rather tied Charlie's stick up and pushed into him, controlling the puck with his feet. His left winger swept by and passed it back to Burnett at the blue line, who skated off to the right, looking for an opening.

So much for getting it into their end, he thought, following Savard to the boards near the red line. Savard wanted to give his smooth-skating teammate some room to operate, and so he stayed to the outside. Zachary hovered at centre waiting to see what Burnett would do. Charlie drifted into the neutral zone to give Zachary some support, all the while keeping a close eye on Savard.

Chelsea's right winger drifted up the boards, and Burnett snapped the puck to him. Zachary moved over to force the winger, who quickly dropped it back to Burnett.

The other Chelsea players took off, including Savard who took a few strides towards the Terrence Falls' end. Burnett took the pass from the winger, and made to fire it across to his defence partner who was up against the far boards. At the last second, however, he changed his mind, faked to his left, and swept to the middle. Zachary came charging off the boards to head him off, lowering his shoulder when he got close, and then, to the surprise of everyone in the arena, knocked Burnett clear off his feet.

The puck sat on the blue line in the middle of the ice. Zachary had fallen, so he couldn't get to it, and neither could Chelsea's right defenceman, who had been camped out at the far boards. Burnett swung his stick wildly as he lay sprawled on the ice, but the puck was out of his reach. That left Charlie and Savard, with Charlie a few feet ahead. Charlie took off like a rocket, gathered up the puck, and moved in for a breakaway. The crowd rose to its feet, oddly quiet, waiting for the drama to unfold before reacting to the sudden turn of events.

Terrence Falls had barely managed a few weak shots the entire first period, so Charlie figured the goalie might be a bit cold. At the hash marks he faked a shot, which froze the goalie for a moment. That was all Charlie needed. The goalie was too far out of his net, and all Charlie had to do was deke to one side and slip the puck in. The goalie realized his mistake quickly, though. Rather than try to get back to his net, he dove forward with a poke check. Charlie moved the puck to his forehand, evading the goalie's stick, but to do that he had to swing wider to his left. That let Savard get close enough to make a play for the puck. Savard swung his stick hard, but instead of hitting Charlie's stick or the puck, he clipped Charlie's left forearm just above the glove. Charlie felt a wave of pain spread up his entire arm to his shoulder. Still, he was able to shovel the puck into the open net before crumpling to his knees, holding his arm with his right hand.

The crowd roared at first, but then quieted quickly when they saw that Charlie was hurt. Charlie felt an arm on his back. To his surprise, it was J.C. Savard, and he looked extremely upset.

"I didn't mean to hit your arm," he said. "I just wanted to knock your stick."

"I think I'm okay," Charlie managed.

That wasn't really true. He was certain his arm was broken. Charlie didn't have a chance to say anything else, because Scott crashed into Savard and sent him flying into his own net. A Chelsea player charged at Scott, and soon a scrum formed.

"What's with the hack job?" Scott screamed at Savard.

The players pushed and shoved each other, while the referees struggled to gain control.

One referee escorted Scott to the penalty box. Pudge skated with Charlie to the bench.

"You're not allowed to get hurt," Pudge said grimly.

"We'll both get through this game — then go to the hospital," Charlie joked to keep his friend from worrying.

When it became clear that only Terrence Falls was getting a penalty, their supporters went berserk, pounding the glass and booing loudly. A few overzealous fans tossed empty cups and popcorn bags onto the ice. Even Hilton had one foot on the edge of the boards and he was yelling at the refs.

"How can you give us a penalty after my guy gets his arm chopped off?"

A referee came over him. "Settle down, or I'll have to give you a penalty for unsportsmanlike conduct."

Hilton flushed, but lowered his voice and stood down from the boards. "Will you at least explain the call to me, please?"

"I had Chelsea's number fourteen for slashing. Then you scored on the delayed penalty, which cancelled the penalty out. Your player charged the Chelsea player after the goal, and I gave him two minutes for roughing."

Hilton didn't give up. "They should get five minutes for attempt to injure. How can you call a minor penalty for that?"

"He didn't try to hurt him. It was just a slash on a breakaway. He isn't that type of player."

"I don't care what type of player he is. I care that he might have broken my captain's arm. And now they get off scot-free, and we're killing a penalty."

The referee shrugged and skated away without responding, pointing to centre for a faceoff. The goal and the slash to Charlie had riled up the crowd. The noise was deafening as the two teams lined up. Terrence Falls had been outplayed to that point, seriously outplayed, and Chelsea had been playing as if it was just a matter of time before they scored. Now that the game was tied up, the Chelsea players looked more serious than they had the whole game to this point. The next goal could decide matters. If Terrence Falls scored, then Chelsea could very easily lose a game that they had been heavily favoured to win.

On the bench, the trainer wrapped an ice pack around Charlie's arm. Tremblay peered over Charlie's shoulder. "Can you move your fingers?"

Charlie wiggled his fingers and nodded.

The trainer probed his arm further, asking Charlie where it hurt. When he pushed the bone on the inside of his left forearm, Charlie winced and pulled back.

"I guess that's the sensitive spot," the trainer joked. "You were lucky, though. The elbow pad absorbed some of the blow. If his stick had hit a bit lower, you probably would have broken a bone. You'll have a nice bruise as a souvenir, but I think that's all."

Hilton came over and asked if Charlie could play.

"He'll be sore tomorrow, but he can play. We'll just wrap it up to give it more protection, and he can go back out there," the trainer said.

"That's what you always say," Hilton grunted. "Let me look." He bent over and examined Charlie's arm.

"It doesn't hurt that much anymore." Charlie wiggled his fingers vigorously to prove the point.

A spasm of pain shot up his arm. His wrist throbbed, but he struggled to hide any sign of discomfort. Without him, they'd be down to Matt at centre — and no one to shadow Savard.

Hilton's eyes narrowed.

"Are you sure you can play?"

"I'm fine, Coach. I just got a stinger, is all."

Hilton bit his upper lip. Finally, he nodded. "We'll give it one shift. Be careful, and we'll monitor the situation."

Matt was coming to the bench calling for a change. Charlie leapt to his feet and hopped the boards before Hilton could change his mind. Nick hit him with a pass almost as soon as his skates touched the ice. He set off down the wing, as the crowd let out a loud cheer when they saw him back on the ice. Charlie was relieved to find that he could grip his stick without too much difficulty. He had no support, up against two defenders, so when he crossed the blue line Charlie fired a shot on net. Instantly, a burning sensation swept down his arm, leaving him feeling sick to his stomach. And even though he'd just come on, and Savard was still on the ice, he headed straight back to the bench.

Fortunately, the pain subsided after icing it for a minute, and he was ready for his next shift. Shooting was definitely out of the question, though. That was not a big problem since his real job was to keep Savard off the score sheet. At the same time, Terrence Falls needed to score to win and, unless he could shoot there was little chance of helping in that department.

Five minutes later the buzzer sounded to end the second period. As he headed off for a change, Savard skated up alongside him and asked about his arm.

"Forget about it," Charlie replied. "It's fine. Just stung, that's all."

"Good," Savard said, tapping Charlie on the shin pads lightly and skating off to his bench.

Charlie sat down next to Pudge. Despite icing it after every shift, his arm had swollen up since taking that shot from the blue line, and one spot on his forearm was still very sensitive, even with the protective bandage. Of course, he wasn't about to let Savard know that. Savard was too good a player not to take advantage if he knew Charlie was playing at less than one hundred percent.

19

LAST MINUTE TO PLAY

With ten minutes to go in the third period, Charlie leaned back and surveyed his teammates on the bench. He realized that on a player-by-player basis, Chelsea was the more talented team. Perhaps Jake, Liam and Thomas would have evened it out, but without them, Terrence Falls simply couldn't match up. As the third period ticked by, Chelsea's skills were taking over, controlling the puck for long stretches of time and showering Alexi with shots. Apart from the occasional icing to relieve the pressure, it seemed the whole game was being played in Terrence Falls' end. Charlie had worked hard to keep the puck off Savard's stick, and the whole team did a good job of containing Burnett, but Chelsea had other players who could play and they were getting closer to scoring.

Constantly defending your own goal is exhausting, and the Terrence Falls players were tired. Charlie knew a tired team made mistakes. He could see it starting too. Instead of playing solid positional hockey, conserving energy, and headmanning the puck, guys began to run around the ice, trying to do things themselves, taking foolish chances with the puck. All were signs of a team in serious trouble. Fortunately, Terrence Falls had an equalizer in Alexi. All champions need great goaltending, and Terrence Falls was getting it, in spades. He was at his best when he got lots of action, thriving on the pressure. Three times in the space of five minutes, a Chelsea player came in on a breakaway, and not one managed to beat the cagey Russian.

Unfortunately, though, despite Alexi's heroics, the inevitable happened. A Chelsea player got loose in front of the net and jammed home a rebound, giving his team the lead. Charlie sensed the energy drain from the entire bench. Shoulders sagged and no one could muster words of encouragement. Even the normally positive Hilton was grim-faced.

"We'll get that back," Charlie announced. "This ain't over. We've come too far to lose. No chance. We gotta get a break at some point."

His fighting words failed to register. His teammates sat quietly and watched the faceoff at centre. Charlie sighed inwardly and took a sip of water. He had tried his best — so had the rest of the team. Sometimes your best wasn't good enough.

"Need liquid?" he offered Pudge.

The plucky right winger had fought through the pain of his swollen ankle to play a mighty game. You couldn't ask more of a teammate — or a friend.

Pudge took a long swig.

"We need one lucky break," Charlie repeated. "The bounces aren't going our way. It's been like that the entire game."

Pudge nodded weakly. His face was pale and drawn.

"You okay to keep playing?" Charlie asked with concern.

Pudge straightened up and placed the water on the ledge in front of him.

"Game's over when the buzzer goes — until then, I'm with you."

Charlie gave Pudge's shoulder pad a whack.

"Then let's tie this game up."

A loud cheer rose from the Terrence Falls supporters.

"What happened?" Charlie asked Zachary.

The left winger stood up, his usual cockeyed grin firmly in place.

"Looks like you got that lucky break. Nick was cuttin' up ice and Chelsea's forechecker got his stick caught in Nick's skates. Cheap penalty — but I say, we'll take it."

Hilton leaned over Charlie's shoulder.

"I agree with Zachary. Why don't you three go out there and get me that goal." In Charlie's ear he whispered, "and I think this is one shift when I want you to ignore Savard and try to score. This could be our last chance with a man advantage. I sense they might be a bit overconfident."

Charlie, Pudge and Zachary filed onto the ice

"This is it, boys," Charlie said to them as they skated to a faceoff just outside Terrence Falls' end. "We may be wounded, but we're not dead yet."

"Not even close," Zachary replied.

"Let's do this," Pudge added.

The referee dropped the puck and Charlie knocked it over to Zachary. Chelsea's left defenceman hadn't moved up to cover him, so Zachary was able to leg it over the red line and fire it into Chelsea's end.

Pudge stormed down his wing after it. He couldn't move too well laterally with his bad foot, but straight ahead he could still bring a load. The defenceman barely touched the puck before Pudge hammered him into the boards with a punishing bodycheck. The puck squirted into the left corner. Charlie went in hard and wrestled it free, shovelling it behind the net to Zachary. Zachary looked around, and fired a sharp pass to Scott at the point. Chelsea set up their box and waited for Terrence Falls to make a move.

Pudge immediately made himself a nuisance. He parked his big frame two feet from the crease and refused to budge an inch, despite several whacks at the back of his legs, courtesy of Chelsea's goalie. Zachary stayed near the boards at the hash marks as an outlet for Scott. Charlie surveyed the scene and, on a whim, went behind Chelsea's net. It took him out of the play, but Chelsea's box was relatively high, and he thought that there might be an opportunity to attack down low.

Maybe it was the cheering crowd, or simply that it can be hard to stay in one place, but the Chelsea winger covering Scott grew impatient, and he suddenly lunged forward, swinging his stick at the puck. Scott was ready.

He bounced to the outside, and fired the puck around the boards to Charlie, who stopped the speeding disk with his body pressed up against the boards. He quickly scooped the puck up and went back behind Chelsea's net.

Now Chelsea had a problem. Neither defenceman could force him to pass for fear of leaving the front of the net open. Chelsea was a well-coached team, however, and didn't panic. Each defenceman covered one post, bending down low to stop the pass in front. The goalie kept back in his net, down on one knee, covering the far post with his pad, and dropping his paddle sideways to the ice. One winger covered Pudge in front of the net, and the other stayed up high to guard the slot.

Charlie feinted left, then right, trying to get Chelsea to overreact, but had no success. He was about to pass it back to the point when Nick charged at the net on the left. Charlie went that way, but the winger up top shifted over to take away the pass. Charlie moved back behind the net. He'd held the puck there for almost ten seconds, and the tension was starting to mount. The crowd was certainly excited, and they roared loudly, imploring their charges on.

Nick remained down low after his little mini-rush at the net. Scott drifted into the centre. Charlie looked up at Scott and nodded. Everything was set up for a play they'd worked on in practice. Charlie rifled a pass to Zachary at the side boards, which drew the left defenceman towards him. Zachary flipped a pass to Scott at the point, and then charged the front of the net to set up a screen with Pudge. Scott raised his stick as if to shoot, which drew the left winger towards him. The two defencemen struggled to push Pudge and Zachary aside, while the other winger watched Nick. That left Charlie still uncovered, and he slipped to the side of the net, behind everyone.

Scott faked the shot and slapped a hard pass to Charlie. Everyone on the ice was completely fooled. The goalie had come out for the shot, and the Chelsea penalty killers were too busy fighting for position in front of the net.

Charlie didn't try to stop the pass. He merely angled his stick and deflected the puck into the net. He spun towards his own goal, and pointed at Scott with his right glove. The two boys embraced in celebration, and were soon joined by Pudge, Zachary and Nick.

"Unbelievable pass," Charlie yelled in Scott's ear.

"Just doing my job, Joyce."

Zachary was pounding his teammates on the helmet. "Beautiful, boys. Way to go. What a play."

The players came to the bench for a change. Hilton was waving at the referee.

"We'll take a time out," he said.

Charlie was surprised. It was odd to call a time out with seven minutes on the clock. Hilton motioned for his team to huddle around.

"Boys, you've played a whale of a game. I'm really proud of you. I don't think anyone in this building expected us to be tied with seven minutes to go." He then added, wryly, "I expected you to be winning, but this is okay.

"I don't want to go end-to-end with them. They've got too many shooters. We need to slow the tempo down and get Chelsea out of its rhythm. If the puck's in our end, ice it. Don't take any chances. When it doubt, fire it up off the glass." He turned to Alexi. "You're the one who can take the most minutes off the clock. Catch every puck you can or cover it up, and hold on unless there's absolutely no one around and the ref is yelling at you to move it."

The referee skated over and blew his whistle. "Time out's over."

"One last thing," Hilton said hurriedly. "When the puck's in their end, only one forechecker. The other two forwards stay outside the zone, either forcing a player with the puck or picking up your check."

The referee's whistle blasted. The Terrence Falls players rushed to set up for the faceoff. Charlie took a seat on the bench. He understood the wisdom of the time out now. The coach realized a new strategy was needed for them to win. The penalty had been a lucky break, and they'd taken advantage. But Chelsea would be coming at them even harder now. Terrence Falls had to slow the game down, or they would certainly give up a goal. If they could frustrate Chelsea, play solid defence and look to counterattack, then they might get lucky and bag the winner.

Matt won the draw, and Ethan slapped it straight up the middle and right on goal. For the next five minutes that scene was repeated over and over. Terrence Falls iced the puck at every opportunity. Chelsea tried to mount an attack, but with four or five Terrence Falls players lined up in the neutral zone, there was little they could do.

The Chelsea fans started booing once they saw Terrence Falls was in a defensive shell. A few began to heckle Hilton.

"Hey, Coach, why don't you just give up?"

"Afraid to play against a real team?"

Charlie grew increasingly uncomfortable with the strategy, and the catcalls stung his pride. Holding back and slowing the game to a crawl went against his competitive nature. He obeyed his coach's orders to the letter, though, along with everyone else, dumping the puck out of their end, icing it, and taking time off the clock at every opportunity.

With a minute to go, the whistle blew. Alexi had robbed Chelsea yet again from point-blank range, with a magnificent glove save.

"Charlie, your line's up," Hilton said. As they filed out the door, he added, "And I think that's enough defensive play for a while. How about we try to win the game?"

Charlie grinned and nodded vigorously. He was more than happy to shift into high gear. His arm was starting to feel better, so he thought he could risk at least one more shot.

Charlie had battled Savard in the faceoff circle all game, and he hadn't done badly. Savard was probably the best centreman he'd ever faced, and whenever he didn't stick to the basics, Savard had beaten him cleanly. Still, an idea came to him. It was risky, but it offered a chance of winning. He guessed Savard would try to draw the puck back to Burnett. His idea was to let Savard win the draw, but intercept the pass before it got to Burnett.

He steeled his nerves and waited for the puck to drop, inching over to Savard's inside shoulder, praying the ref wouldn't notice and tell him to square up. Fortunately, the ref was more focused on making sure everyone lined up outside the circle. When the players were all set to his satisfaction, he bent down, held the puck over their sticks momentarily, and dropped it.

Charlie hesitated for a fraction of a second. Savard drew the puck back, but didn't notice that Charlie had jumped around him until it was too late. Burnett never got to let that big shot go. Instead, Charlie got the puck first. He veered away from Burnett towards the boards. The other defenceman made a bad decision and tried a poke check at the blue line. Charlie simply bounced the puck off the boards, skated around the defender, and picked it up just inside the red line.

Charlie raced down the ice on the left side. He glanced over his right shoulder and spotted Zachary striding up fast to catch him. Burnett had managed to scramble back, skating backwards frantically, looking back and forth between the two attackers. Charlie slowed to allow Zachary to catch up. They hit the blue line together. Charlie slid the puck to Zachary, who immediately turned on the jets to the outside. Burnett was surprised by the move. It looked as if Zachary had forgotten that it was a two-on-one. Zachary surprised him even more when he cut in sharply towards the net at the hash marks. The goalie moved out to protect the short side, and Burnett slid along the ice to block what he thought would be a shot on goal. The rangy winger had not forgotten Charlie at all, however. At the last moment, he flicked a pass across to Charlie in the slot. The goalie flung himself back to the middle of the net in a butterfly. Charlie took one stride with the puck and from ten feet out snapped the puck decisively. His arm hurt when he let it go, but he didn't hold anything back.

Clank!

The goalie's best friend came to Chelsea's rescue — the sound of it broke Charlie's heart. The puck rang off the crossbar and ricocheted straight back to Savard, who whirled around to lead a counterattack.

Savard hadn't had much of an opportunity to skate in open ice since the first shift of the game when he missed the breakaway, so he clearly wanted to make the most of it now. He fired a crisp pass to his left winger, who wisely passed it back once Savard had gathered up a good head of steam. The crowd was really into it now, sensing that this might be the deciding moment.

Savard bore down on Scott and Nick. They both readied themselves at the blue line, determined to stand him up. Savard veered towards Scott and faked a move outside — the steady defenceman didn't bite. He kept his eyes directly on Savard's chest, and waited for him to make a real move. And that he did. When he was five feet away, Savard cut into the middle of the ice and pushed the puck between them. Nick lowered his shoulder, and Scott bent down for a hip check.

They never got to deliver the hit, however. Savard jumped right over Scott's hip, causing him to miss entirely and slam into Nick. That knocked Nick off-stride, and he was only able to get a piece of Savard, which wasn't enough to knock him down. Savard landed on his feet and calmly collected the puck, as the two Terrence Falls defencemen crashed to the ice. Savard shifted the puck to his forehand, then to his backhand. Alexi moved out, challenging him to shoot. When he was eight feet away, Savard answered that challenge, firing the puck into the top right corner just over Alexi's blocker.

Charlie didn't see the goal. He had his head down the whole way back, skating as hard as he could, praying that Savard would miss. The roar of the crowd told him his prayer had not been answered. He slumped over, resting his stick on his knees and glided back to his end. If his shot had only been one inch lower, they'd be celebrating, not Chelsea.

Chelsea's entire squad flooded onto the ice, mobbing their star and captain, pounding him on the head and high-fiving each other. The referee blew his whistle, and skated over to remind them that there was still time on the clock. That broke up the celebrations, although they carried on to the Chelsea bench, and their fans certainly kept up the cheering. Hilton waved for Charlie's line to stay on. Charlie won the draw easily, Savard content to hang back and help protect Chelsea's slender lead. Now it was his turn to cover Charlie. Scott gobbled up the puck, skated it to the red line, and dumped it in.

Alexi raced to the bench to allow for an extra attacker. Matt came over the boards to replace him and charged towards Chelsea's end. He may as well have saved his energy. Burnett got to the puck first, evaded Pudge's effort to forecheck, and skated out of his own end. When Matt bore down on him, Burnett just slid the puck softly down the side, careful not to get an icing.

Nick raced back to retrieve the puck. The clock was down to thirty seconds. His desperate pass to Zachary on the right side was intercepted and sent right back into their end. Nick gathered it up behind the net and headed up ice. Savard forechecked aggressively, which forced Nick to pass it to Charlie, who in turn spun and fired it into Chelsea's end.

Again, Burnett was there first. He lofted a high backhand over everyone's heads. It landed at Savard's feet, near centre. The slick goal scorer didn't try for an empty-netter. Instead, he danced around with the puck, running down the clock. When the buzzer sounded, he slapped the puck off the boards and threw his stick and gloves high into the air, racing back to his goalie. The rest of his teammates did the same. Chelsea had won the tournament.

Crestfallen, the Terrence Falls squad drifted to their end to console Alexi.

"We were only in the game because of you," Charlie said, wrapping his arm around the distraught goalie.

"Couldn't catch a break this game," Nick added.

"Garbage goal," Alexi declared. "I should've had it. Went down too soon. Next time, there's no way I'll let it in."

"Let's line up," Charlie said. "They deserved it. Nothing to be ashamed of."

He led the team to centre ice, removing his glove to shake hands. They had to wait for a minute, though, because the Chelsea players were still congratulating each other. Their coach finally noticed, and he instructed the players to shake hands. J.C. Savard was first in line. He'd taken his helmet off. His long, blond hair was plastered to his forehead. With a good-natured grin, he swung his hand out to meet Charlie's.

"You gave us a serious battle. It was fun playing you."

"You deserved to win. We just couldn't get control of the puck."

"How's the arm?"

"It would feel better if we'd won."

Savard laughed and held out his hand to Pudge. The crowd cheered for both teams loudly. It had been a great, entertaining and clean game, and they clapped to show their appreciation. Once the teams finished shaking hands, they lined up on their respective blue lines for the medal ceremony.

Like any true athlete, Charlie hated to lose. Losing in the finals was the worst feeling — to come so close and then not make it. Almost as painful was being forced to stay on the ice and watch Chelsea get their gold medals. He heard his name called out, and went to accept his silver medal.

"Ladies and gentlemen," the announcer said. "Let's hear it for the winners of the Champions Cup, junior division — the Chelsea Spartans." He held the trophy up over his head, and then added, "And this is the sixth year in a row that Chelsea's junior team has won. Now that's a dynasty!"

The crowd clapped and cheered loudly. A few of the Chelsea players banged their sticks on the ice, while others waved at the crowd. Scott leaned over to Charlie and Nick.

"If I'd known how irritating this would be, I would've tried harder."

"I can't believe I hit the crossbar," Charlie replied. "I just can't believe it."

"I swear the crossbar moved," Nick snorted. "It was going right in, and the crossbar moved."

The announcer interrupted them.

"We have a final presentation to make — most valuable player. Let's hear it for Chelsea's captain, the tournament's leading goal scorer, point getter, and now the holder of the record for most points in the junior division in one tournament — J.C. Savard."

Another loud cheer went up. Charlie joined in, slapping his stick on the ice. Savard had played hard but fair

— the way hockey should be played.

Savard held the MVP trophy over his head, skating back to his teammates. They mobbed their captain, emphatically agreeing with the MVP decision.

The Terrence Falls squad left the ice first, relieved that the presentations were over. The jubilant Chelsea team stayed on for a few more minutes, to take a team picture, and to continue to enjoy their victory.

20

FEELS LIKE HOME

The mood became surprisingly upbeat once Charlie's teammates got into their dressing room. They'd lost, and in heartbreaking fashion, but they'd also given the mighty Chelsea a good run for its money, with three key players gone, not to mention Pudge's ankle and Charlie's arm. Most of the guys started joking around, throwing tape balls at each other, and rehashing the game. Charlie took no part in the horseplay. The loss was still too fresh in his mind. To win the Champions Cup, after Jake, Liam and Thomas quitting, would have been so sweet.

The two coaches had been shaking hands with all their players, offering praise and words of encouragement. They stopped in front of Charlie.

"Cheer up, son," Tremblay said. "That was one of the gutsiest efforts I've seen, and after forty years of coaching I've seen my share."

Charlie forced a smile. "The team played great," he said.

"Losing always hurts more than winning feels

good," Hilton said. "If that ever changes, it's time to stop playing. And you can take pride in the fact that you did what no one else has done — stop Savard."

"I don't know about that. He scored the winning goal."

The coaches laughed. "We'll chalk that up to bad luck," Hilton said. "What a bizarre goal, the way the puck bounced straight back. What can you do? I guess it wasn't meant to be."

He offered his hand. "Put 'er there, captain."

He and Charlie shook hands.

"You're a tremendous player, Charlie," Tremblay said, shaking hands with him next. "I've enjoyed working with you."

"Thanks," Charlie said, feeling slightly overwhelmed.

Hilton moved to the middle of the room. "Can I interrupt everyone for a second. I just wanted to say a few words before you all go.

"I'm not going to give you the old 'We tried hard and I'm proud of you' speech, even though you did and I am. This game showed two things. First, what you can accomplish with an honest effort and discipline. We played with heart, and we played with our heads. No dumb penalties — no dumb mistakes."

"Except for hitting the crossbar," Scott wisecracked, tossing a tape ball at Charlie.

"You might have a point there," Hilton said. "You all played as well as you could. Each one of you can take pride in that. The second thing this game showed is that you can improve. There are no more school games until next year, but I trust you are all going to play for a club team this winter. We were a bit outmatched today in the skills department. I hope you use this as motivation to get better."

He took a sip of water from a bottle he was holding. "Silver is still a precious metal," he said, "and a bunch of other teams would gladly change places with you."

He glanced at his watch. "The senior team is playing in their final right now. I'm sorry to report that the junior girls also lost in the final. The senior girls team lost in the semis. I'm hoping we can get at least one gold. Once you get dressed, maybe some of you will want to stay and watch with Coach Tremblay and me. We'll be in the stands."

Coach Tremblay clapped his hands, as if to applaud the team's efforts. "Thanks for letting me coach you guys. I had a lot of fun, and I think you did too. Tough loss. Hate to lose in the finals, but remember one thing: it's better to lose the big one than to watch it."

He gave them a wave and left with Hilton. The players finished dressing quickly, eager to get out to see their senior team, led by Karl Schneider, do what they could not — beat Chelsea. The two teams were evenly matched and both had sailed into the finals undefeated.

"No way they can shut down Schneider. He's been a scoring machine — twelve goals in four games, and no one has even come close to stopping him," Pudge said to Charlie.

"One guy can't win a game," Charlie said.

"We'll just have to see about that."

"Hey, Charlie, you ready?" Scott asked.

"Yeah. Hold on. You comin', Pudge?"

"Go ahead. I'll be out in a sec."

Charlie left with Scott and Nick. He spotted his family waiting for him by the snack bar. Danielle was munching on some popcorn, while his grandparents were sipping on coffees. He told his friends to go on ahead, and went over to them. Danielle saw him first and waved excitedly. He was carrying his bag and stick with his right arm, so he waved back with his left hand without thinking. A sharp stab of pain reminded him of his injury. He'd been icing his arm on the bench. Now that he wasn't doing that, it was beginning to throb. His mother saw him grimace when he waved, and immediately rushed over, deep concern etched in her face. She touched his arm gently and asked how it felt.

"It hurts a bit," he admitted. Charlie didn't want to worry his mother. And he really wanted to watch the game. "I can move my fingers, so it's probably fine."

"Thanks, Doctor Charlie," his mother said, taking hold of his arm. "How about I take a quick look anyway?"

She rolled up his sleeve and began to probe his arm gently with her fingertips. A very large bruise had already formed midway up his forearm. She shook her head and sighed. "You probably didn't break it, or you couldn't have held your stick. It's hard to tell, though. You've got a lot of swelling. If you're lucky you'll only have a deep bruise. You could have chipped a bone, though. Either way, we'd better get you to Emergency for an x-ray and have it checked out."

Charlie's shoulders slumped. He really wanted to see that game. "Can't I just stay for a little while? It really doesn't hurt that much. I was able to play with it. And a lot of the guys are staying to watch the senior finals between Terrence Falls and Chelsea." His voice trailed off and he cast a pleading look at his mother.

"You could have a broken arm," she said firmly. "What if you need a cast? It's important to get it looked at right away. I should add that I've been hanging out in an arena the entire weekend, and I really don't feel like watching another game. So let's go, please."

"It's just for an hour," he tried.

"Charlie, I realize you want to watch, but I'm sorry. We have to go to the hospital."

Just then, Pudge limped over.

"Hey, Charlie. You're gonna miss the whole game. Schneider's totally out of control. He almost scored in the first minute. Went through the whole Chelsea team and rang one off the post. It's going to be an awesome game. Your family can tell you how great you played later."

Charlie introduced Pudge.

"It's nice to finally meet you," Charlie's mother said.

"Nice to meet you too," Pudge said.

"I wouldn't mind watching the game," Danielle said. "I've still got some popcorn and a slushie to finish."

"Aren't you going to watch?" Pudge asked

"My mom wants me to go to the hospital."

"My dad's taking me after the game for my foot," Pudge said. "It's swollen up again, so he thinks I might have done some real damage. I'm sure it's fine — just needs some ice. We could take you."

"How about it, Mom? It can't get any worse — and I promise not to clap too hard."

Charlie's mother smiled, and she patted his arm softly. "Oh, all right. But I may as well stay and watch too. One more game won't kill me."

"Thanks, Mom," he said.

Some of the guys saw Pudge and Charlie and they waved at them to come over. Scott was on his feet, trading friendly insults with the Chelsea fans. His natural good humour couldn't be dampened by the loss of a hockey game. His friends were laughing at his jokes, egging him on. It suddenly occurred to Charlie that while he'd only known Scott for a short time, it felt as if they'd been friends forever. After Pudge, Scott had been the first guy to make him feel welcome in Terrence Falls, starting with asking him to join his group for that skating drill at the first tryout. He'd proven to be a loyal friend. Charlie vowed to himself he'd never forget that.

Nick sat next to Scott. His jacket was completely open, despite it being quite cold in the stands. The cold didn't seem to bother him. It took a lot to bother Nick, Charlie mused. He was that kind of guy. If something went wrong on the ice, he just put it behind him and kept on going. He may not be the easiest guy to get to know. He rarely talked about himself — the opposite of Scott. But you always knew where you stood with Nick.

That's what he liked best about him. Charlie was proud to count him as a friend.

Charlie and Pudge squeezed in beside Zachary. Charlie reflected on how much things had changed for Pudge in only a few weeks. He'd stood up to Jake, Liam and Thomas. That took true courage. Pudge had also proven his courage on the ice, thriving in his new position, always willing to dig hard in the corner, always ready to sacrifice the body — and he'd just played an entire game on a badly injured foot. And Charlie would always remember that moment when Pudge nominated him for captain. At the time he'd thought it was the worst possible thing that could have happened. Now he knew that it was the best. He had a feeling that Pudge and he would be friends for a long time to come.

Zachary was treating the stands like a lounge chair — his legs were draped over the seat in front and his hands were folded behind his head. That was Zachary — laid back, without a worry in the world. Some people thought he didn't care about things. Charlie knew that wasn't true. He was a fierce competitor — he put more into the game today than most. He just didn't let things get to him. Charlie envied his ability to do that. He was also a very talented player, covering huge tracks of ice with his long, rangy stride, always seeming to be in the right place at the right time. He complemented Charlie's style perfectly. Charlie hoped he'd have the chance to play with him again.

And there was Matt, sitting in a row behind Scott and Nick. He was watching the game, listening to Scott rant, laughing with the others, but it looked to Charlie like he wasn't really comfortable hanging out with these guys. That was understandable. Jake, Liam and Thomas had been his buddies for years. They'd gone to the same schools, been in the same classes, and played on the same hockey teams. Now he'd very definitely turned his back on all that. It was incredible to think how much things had changed since that fateful day when he'd bodychecked Matt in practice during the one-on-one drill. Charlie had grown to respect Matt tremendously. He was obviously someone who thought for himself. He'd also had a great game playing in a different position, often double-shifting so Charlie could match up with Savard. He never complained once. He just dug deep and kept working.

The score was tied at 1–1, with the action swinging from end to end, neither team much interested in playing defensively. The pain in his arm was soon forgotten in all the excitement. Charlie cheered wildly with all the Terrence Falls supporters when a minute before the end of the first period, Karl Schneider scored the go-ahead goal on a beautiful wraparound from behind Chelsea's net.

While Scott led a chant of "Ter-rence Falls", Charlie tried to put everything that had happened since he arrived in this town in perspective. It was hard, because so much had happened in such a short period of time. It felt as if he'd been in Terrence Falls for years instead of weeks. He had to admit that Terrence Falls was home now, and it wasn't that bad a place to be. He would always miss his old home — and things weren't perfect here. It would always feel weird being here without his dad. Somehow, though, Charlie knew this was the best place for him to be right now.

He elbowed Pudge gently in the ribs. "I just need to talk to Matt for a second. Save my seat."

He walked up the stairs and slipped in beside Matt.

"How's the arm?" Matt asked.

"It's killing me, but there's no way I'm missing this game."

"Good school spirit."

They settled down to watch the game.

Matt turned to him with a serious expression. "So what club team are you going to play for?" he asked abruptly.

Charlie shrugged and shook his head. "Not really sure," he answered. "I haven't given it much thought. I know tryouts were held back in the spring, so there aren't many spots left. What team do you play on?"

"I used to play for the Wildcats," Matt said, "but that's who Jake, Liam and Thomas play with. I guess we're both in the same situation. We should test the free agent market and see what comes up."

Then Matt pointed to Scott, Nick, Pudge and Zachary. With a lopsided grin, he proposed, "Maybe we should all try to find a team together?"

The horn sounded ending the first period.

"Maybe that's a very good idea," Charlie replied.

He rose with his friends to cheer Terrence Falls, as the teams switched ends for the second period.

Want to read more about Charlie Joyce
and his teammates?

Turn the page for an excerpt from

the exciting second book in the
Game Time series!

1

CLOSE CALL

Charlie readied himself for the shot.

"Eat some yellow tennis ball," the shooter said, and he launched a blistering slapshot.

Partly screened by two players, Charlie threw out his arm in desperation. The ball nicked the blocker and deflected up over his shoulder.

Clunk!

It hit the crossbar and bounced back in front of the net. Four players scrambled madly for it. Charlie dropped into a butterfly to protect the lower half of the net. The shooter got control of the ball and cut hard to the far post. Out of position, Charlie sprawled on his back and held up his catcher.

Whack.

The shooter banged his stick on the pavement. He'd fired it right into Charlie's glove. Charlie laughed as he got to his feet. Talk about lucky saves!

"Admit it — that was highway robbery," the shooter demanded.

"Not my fault you can't score on an open net, Scott," Charlie replied.

He took off his goalie mask. He was tired — they'd

been playing for two hours — but he wasn't about to stop. It was tough enough to even get his friends to play road hockey. The hockey season had started a week ago, and now they were all too busy to hang out. That was life, he supposed. It wouldn't be so bad if he played for a team too, but he hadn't arrived in Terrence Falls until the beginning of the school year, so he'd missed the spring tryouts.

"I'll give you dudes one more chance to score on me," he said.

Charlie curled his stick around the ball and flicked it down the driveway. It bounced between Scott's legs and rolled down the driveway all the way to the other side of the street.

Scott rolled his eyes. "Great, Joyce. Now someone has to get it back."

"I'm just trying to get you in shape for the hockey season," Charlie said. "So be a good boy and fetch."

Instead, Scott walked over to the front lawn and flopped to the grass. "I'm starving. Any of you hiding a burger and fries in his pocket?" he said. "Pudge, did you bring any goodies from your dad's restaurant?"

"Sorry, Scott. I thought you might last a few minutes without eating."

"A few minutes — are you insane?"

"Does your new coach know about your weight problem?" Nick asked.

"What weight problem?"

"You'll see," Nick said.

Scott threw a clump of dirt in reply, which Nick avoided by dropping to the ground.

"I have an old sandwich in my knapsack," Nick said.

"It's from two days ago and I might've dropped it on the ground a few times, but . . ."

"I can't believe you've been holding out on me," Scott said. "I thought we were friends. Fork it over."

"Make me."

"We'll settle it like men — thumb wrestle! Two out of three."

"I got my money on Nick," Zachary called out.

"Ten bucks on Scott," Pudge said.

They obviously didn't want to play street hockey anymore. But Charlie wasn't in the mood to joke around.

"I'll see what we've got in the kitchen," Charlie said quietly.

When he went inside, he found his mom washing the floor.

"Stop right there, young man," she said. "I don't want you dragging your dirty shoes all over."

"Sorry, Mom. Just wondered if there was something to munch. Some of the guys — well, Scott, actually — are kind of hungry."

His mom laughed. "I swear that boy eats enough to feed ten people."

"He won the school hot dog eating contest — ten in only five minutes, including the bun. A new record."

"Very impressive. Give me a few minutes for the floor to dry and I'll dig something up."

"Thanks, Mom . . . and we don't need anything special. Chips or something would be cool."

"Charlie, I have a reputation to uphold. It wouldn't look good for a café owner to serve junk food."

"Don't worry about it — keep it simple."

"Leave it to me."

He knew there was no point arguing, so he left. He was proud of his mom. She'd only opened her café a month ago, and it was already doing great. She was a really good cook. Still, it was embarrassing when friends came over and she baked cookies or a cake, as if he was still a little kid.

When he went outside, Scott and Nick were balancing on their heads. Zachary and Pudge were cheering them on. "What're they up to now?" Charlie said.

"Thumb war didn't settle it," Pudge said. "They've moved on to a headstand competition."

"Hey, Zachary, how was practice today?" Charlie asked.

"Kinda cool. A power skating coach who once tried out for the Chicago Blackhawks had us doing all sorts of intense drills. Major tempo. I was totally wiped out by the end."

"How's the team look?"

Zachary shrugged. "We have a solid crew. The Snow Birds won the championship last year, and I guess we're favoured to win again. The Wildcats are supposed to be good too."

He couldn't help feeling a bit jealous. Zachary made it sound as if playing for the Snow Birds was no big deal. But that was Zachary — he was laid back about everything.

"What about you, Pudge? You changed your mind about the Wildcats?" he asked.

"Are you kidding? No way I'd play with Jake — not to mention Liam and Thomas. And Coach Schultz is too over the top. He was always on my case, ranting about something or other. I was on that team for two years — two years too many, as far as I'm concerned."

He understood about not wanting to play with Jake and his friends. They'd bullied Pudge for years, and had made Charlie's life miserable from the first day of school. He was one happy camper when they transferred from his homeroom. He did owe them one thing, though. He had become friends with Pudge because of their bullying. They had stood up to them together. Charlie thought of Pudge as his best friend, though he doubted Pudge thought the same — they'd only met a month ago. Pudge wasn't funny like Scott, or a terrific athlete like Nick, or cool like Zachary. He was just someone you could trust. At least he and Pudge could hang together a bit since neither of them had a team.

"I've called around to all the triple-A and double-A teams — I couldn't even get a tryout," Charlie said. "Have you heard of anything lately?"

Pudge reddened slightly. "Forgot to tell you. The Tornadoes invited me out. My dad knows the coach . . . from the restaurant . . . and . . . well . . . I signed with them." He cleared his throat and looked down at the ground before continuing. "I asked if they had a spot for you." He shrugged. "Coach said they were full up."

"Great. I'm the only guy without a team."

Charlie instantly regretted his words. He sounded angry, and Pudge was clearly embarrassed. But Pudge hadn't done anything wrong. He had a right to play.

Scott ran over with his arms over his head.

"All hail the headstand champion of the world. Bow before me, mortals."

Nick was right behind. "He lies."

Scott flashed a grin. "Maybe I didn't exactly win. But Nick cheats and everyone knows it." He put his arm around Charlie's shoulders. "So where's that grub?"

"It's coming. My mom's on it."

"Awesome. I hope she brings those chocolate chip cookies," Scott said.

"I'm hoping for the raspberry tarts," Nick said.

"The ones with the whipped cream around the edges?" Scott said. "Those babies rock."

"Tell me about your team," Charlie said, "to take your mind off your stomach."

Scott stretched out on the grass, and put his hands behind his head. "The Hornets will be the team to beat, no doubt. We've got two good goalies. And, with me on defence, the blue line is solid — naturally. And we got a couple of guys up front with skills."

"You told me you've got practically the same lineup as last year," Nick said.

"We do."

"The Hornets finished three points out of last place."

"New season — new attitude."

"Same players — same results."

Pudge interrupted. "I bet Charlie would be able to help you guys."

Scott's tone grew serious. "I asked the coach. He told me the league only allows him to sign seventeen players, and he'd already committed back in April. He did say that if someone drops out he'd love to have you. Tough spot to be in, Joyce. I mean, after how well you played in the Champions Cup last month for our school team, I figured you'd be a lock for a triple-A spot."

"I'm not sweating it too much," Charlie said bravely. "I bet something will come up. I may not play competitive hockey this season, but that's cool. I'll just be ready for the spring tryouts for next season."

It killed him to think that — but he wasn't going to be a whiner.

"I'm here for you if you need a good cry," Scott said.

That earned him a clump of dirt from each of the guys.

Charlie stood to take off his pads. His father had given them to him two years ago. The insides were all worn, and the lining at the bottom was coming apart. They were also too short. Scott had blasted a shot off his ankle, and he could feel the bruise coming up. He'd never think of getting new ones, though. He'd rather suffer a thousand bruises. He didn't have many things left to remind him of his father.

He fought a wave of bitterness. It was still hard to think about his father dying in that car accident.

"No better feeling than taking off goalie pads," Charlie said, holding one up.

Scott grinned. "It's a good look for you. Gives you that ultra-dope waddle when you walk."

"Show me." Charlie tossed the pad at him.

"Chawie! Chawie! Josh have ball. Josh fwo ball."

Charlie looked up and felt his heart rise to his throat. His three-year-old neighbour from across the street was standing in the middle of the road, holding a ball and giggling — totally oblivious to the car racing towards him!

"Josh, car!" Charlie screamed.

Josh froze and dropped the ball. Charlie felt things happen in slow motion, as if he were watching himself in a movie. With one goalie pad still on, he ran towards Josh, scooped him up in his left arm and catapulted himself towards the curb. They tumbled to the road. Josh began to shriek, thrashing and kicking.

"You're okay," Charlie said. "It's over." A wave of relief washed over him.

"Joshie! Joshie! Are you all right? Are you hurt?"

"I think he's good, Mr. Hume," Charlie said.

Josh ran to his father and jumped into his arms.

Charlie hadn't known his neighbours long, but he'd noticed how Mr. Hume doted on his son. They were always together. It had been like that with his own dad.

Josh stopped crying.

By this time his friends had surrounded him.

"You guys good?" Pudge asked.

Charlie nodded.

"That was fun," Josh said, which made everyone laugh.

"Hume! What kind of parent are you?"

It was the driver. Charlie got to his feet and slid over to join his friends. He found the guy kind of intimidating. He was tall and well built, and his eyes had dark circles underneath that gave him a menacing appearance. His clothes looked expensive. Charlie couldn't stop looking at his enormous gold watch. It covered almost his entire wrist. He'd never seen a watch like that.

He looked over at Mr. Hume, whose face had flushed deeply. Mr. Hume lowered his eyes and shrugged.

"I was washing the car,' he said weakly. "Guess I took my eyes off Josh for a second, Mr. Dunn."

"Pay attention," he replied. "Little kid like that — you can't let them out of your sight. Lucky I hit the brakes in time. Not many drivers have my reaction time."

"I'm grateful," Mr. Hume said.

Charlie didn't buy that. Dunn was speeding — and he hadn't hit the brakes fast enough. In fact, Charlie was pretty sure he'd been talking on a cell phone.

Dunn crouched down in front of Josh. "You watch yourself, little buddy. Promise me there'll be no more running onto the street."

Josh hid behind his dad's legs.

Dunn grunted and stood up. "That reminds me," he said. "Hume, get to the store early tomorrow, around seven. We have a new shipment of hockey gear to organize."

"I'll be there, Mr. Dunn." He cleared his throat. "See you then. I think I'll take Josh inside." He picked up Josh and turned to go. "Thanks," he whispered as he passed Charlie.

"Bye, Chawie," Josh said, over his dad's shoulder.

The boys gathered together. Dunn put his hands on his hips. Charlie wished he'd leave. He made things weird.

"Don't some of you attend Terrence Falls High School?"

No one answered for a few moments.

"We all do," Charlie said finally.

Dunn swung around and looked right at Charlie.

"My son goes there — Mike Dunn. You know him?"

Charlie nodded. "We're all in grade nine with Mike."

"Any of you hockey players?"

This time they all nodded.

"Are you any good?"

Charlie exchanged looks with his friends. How were they supposed to answer that? Fortunately, they didn't have to. Dunn continued without waiting for a reply.

"You're all minor bantam age, so this may be of interest — that's if you can really play. The triple-A division of the East Metro Hockey League is about to change forever. The Aeros lost their sponsor about a week ago and had to pack it in. They've never done much anyway. I don't think the league was too heartbroken that they folded. Anyway, the league went looking for a replacement team — and yours truly answered the call."

Charlie had spoken to the Aeros' coach. At least this explained why he'd been so vague about a tryout.

Dunn continued. "I've always thought about taking over a team — grabbing the helm and building a winner — a powerhouse. So that's just what I'm gonna do. And believe me, when I decide to do something — I do it. Nothing stands in my way. That's what got me where I am today."

Charlie had never heard anyone speak with such confidence.

"How many players are you looking for?" Charlie asked.

"I've already signed a few. But I need at least ten more solid players — guys with real potential and the right attitude. If you guys think you fit the bill, give it a shot. Tryouts start in two days. Team's called the Hawks. Take my card and give me a call if you're interested."

He gave a bunch of cards to Charlie, flipped his keys in his hand, winked, and went back to his car. The engine roared and he set off at high speed, the tires screeching as he pulled away. No one said a word until he was out of sight.

He looked at the card: *Tom Dunn, President, Dunn's Sportsmart.*

"Charlie, I have one question," Scott said. "When did you have time to find a phone booth and change into your Superman costume before saving that kid?"

He didn't answer.

"Joyce?" Scott prompted.

"Umm . . . I don't know." He was too excited by the news to listen. It was perfect — a AAA team in Terrence Falls with ten open spots. That meant he had a shot at playing competitive hockey this season — or, better yet, they could all play for the Hawks! That would be way cool. Hockey was practically the most important thing in his life. It was the only thing that had made things bearable after his father died and they moved to Terrence Falls. And now, out of nowhere, some guy decides to sponsor a brand-new team. It was like a miracle.

"Can you believe it?" Charlie said. "Isn't it too bizarre for words?"

"Is what too bizarre for words?" Pudge asked.

They were all staring at him. Didn't they get it?

"The Hawks . . . the new team. We could all play together. It would be like the school team — only better, because instead of just playing a weekend tournament, we'd be on the same team for a whole season. We almost won the Champion's Cup — we could even give the Snow Birds a serious battle."

No one said a word. He wondered what they were thinking.

"I never thought of it that way," Pudge said. "It's an interesting idea, I guess."

"It's more than interesting," he responded. "It's, like, totally interesting. It's, like, over-the-top interesting. What could be—"

Nick interrupted. "What about the commitments we signed? It seems a bit bogus to quit two weeks before the start of the regular season."

They walked back to the lawn. What could he say to that? He searched his brain for an answer.

"Nick, I see your point. On the other hand, this is a once-in-a-lifetime opportunity. Sure, we can all play on separate teams, play it safe this year. But I say, take a chance and play together. Think about the school team. Pudge and Zachary, we could be on the same line again. Scott and Nick, you could be defence partners again."

"My dad would kill me after he made all those calls to the other coaches," Pudge said.

Scott and Nick seemed deep in thought. Charlie turned to Zachary.

"I know giving up a spot on the Snow Birds is tough. They've got an awesome lineup. But that team is stacked. You'd just be another player. On the Hawks you'd be a star and get twice the ice time. It'd be cool to have you on my wing. I bet we'd lead the league in goals."

Zachary nodded, but didn't say anything. He looked away.

This was going nowhere. Maybe Pudge . . .

"How about my left winger?"

Pudge returned his gaze for a moment. Charlie grew hopeful. There was something about the look in his eye.

"It is an interesting idea, I guess," Pudge said.

Not exactly an over-the-top reaction — better than a no, at least.

"Maybe you guys can think about it. I'm gonna take a shot and, well . . . it'll be cool either way. We can play on the same team or against each other. I wouldn't mind dangling Scott with the puck a few times."

"Science fiction, Joyce," Scott said. "I'm too inside your head to fall for your bogus moves. But wait till you play Nick. He tends to wet himself and get distracted."

Nick pretended to be horrified. "I thought you weren't gonna tell the boys about that . . . problem."

"No secrets among friends — although I kinda put that on Facebook," Scott said.

Nick shrugged. "As long as it's only all the kids at school."

They started cracking jokes about how their teams stacked up against each other. Charlie couldn't really join in. The Hawks weren't even a team yet. The conversation gave him a chance to think about it, however. The Hawks gave him a real chance to play in the top league after all, and maybe Pudge would switch since he didn't know guys on his team. Matt was also looking for a team. He used to play for the Wildcats, and since the school tournament he'd become a friend. Matt didn't like Jake any more than Charlie or Pudge did. He had to accept that Scott, Nick and Zachary probably wouldn't leave established teams — especially Zachary.

The Snow Birds were a dynasty.

"Anyone hungry?" his mom called out.

Scott leapt to his feet.

"There's enough for everyone," his mom laughed.

"Not if I eat it all first," Scott replied, racing up the steps into the house.

"I'll give you a call later to talk about the Hawks," Charlie said to Pudge as they followed.

Pudge nodded, but didn't say anything.

Charlie could have punched himself. The guy was obviously not into it. It was stupid to expect anyone to quit a team just to play with him. Plain dumb. He needed to be cool about it. It would be enough just to make the Hawks.

Charlie forced himself to grin and he laughed along with the others as Scott struggled to stuff two bananas into his mouth on a dare from Nick.

ABOUT THE AUTHOR

David Skuy spent most of his childhood playing one sport or another — hockey, soccer, football, rugby. Now he is a writer and lawyer who lives in Toronto, Ontario with his wife and two kids. He still plays hockey once a week and remains a die-hard Leafs fan.

He began writing the Game Time series to try to capture the competition, the challenges, the friendships and the rivalries that make sports so much fun.

The Game Time series:

Off the Crossbar
Rebel Power Play